"Kissing you was pure instinct."

Curt spoke in a perfectly cool voice. "Up to now, it's an instinct I've wrestled down. It didn't seem right. Sweet little Rachael Munro. You may have done a terrible thing by reminding me you're twenty-three."

"More likely, kissing me was all part of your grand plan," Rachael said, equally cool. "Sonia might fall on your every word. I can't be so easily manipulated, Curt."

"But of course you *can*," he said in a compelling, ferociously sexy voice.

"I guess I deserved that," Rachael sighed.

"Don't worry, I'm no predator feasting on little girls like you. After all, I remember you when you were just a kid."

"And I remember you striding all around the place with your father. You had this tremendous air of being lord of all you surveyed. I used to think it was one of your attractions. Now I'm not so sure...."

Margaret Way is known for her passionate romances and for her wonderfully lyrical descriptions of Australia. She was born and educated in the river city of Brisbane and now lives within sight and sound of beautiful Moreton Bay in the state of Queensland. She delights in bringing her homeland alive for readers.

Prior to beginning her writing career, Margaret had a musical one—she was a pianist, teacher, vocal coach and accompanist. She still plays the piano seriously; she also collects art and antiques and is devoted to her garden.

Margaret Way's first romance was published almost twenty-five years ago—in 1970—and she very quickly became a favorite with readers. She has plans and ideas for many more novels!

Books by Margaret Way

HARLEQUIN ROMANCE
2832—DIAMOND VALLEY
2939—MORNING GLORY
2958—DEVIL MOON
2976—MOWANA MAGIC
2999—THE HUNGRY HEART
3295—ONE FATEFUL SUMMER

THE CARRADINE BRAND
Margaret Way

Harlequin Books

TORONTO • NEW YORK • LONDON
AMSTERDAM • PARIS • SYDNEY • HAMBURG
STOCKHOLM • ATHENS • TOKYO • MILAN
MADRID • WARSAW • BUDAPEST • AUCKLAND

To Bernie Stevenson,
with thanks

ISBN 0-373-03331-1

THE CARRADINE BRAND

CHAPTER ONE

THE PITILESS SUN drove them to make camp, hot, tired, covered in sweat. They had been on the go since sunup, flushing out the man-shy cleanskins from the scrub near Devil's Gorge. Eerie country, always quivering and pulsing in the quicksilver light of mirage. Very rough in parts, it was an ideal sanctuary for the cattle, with its deep pockets of food-bearing bush and a network of multicolored gullies—amethyst, orange, sapphire and rose-pink. Even in the times of greatest drought, the gullies held puddles of life-giving water.

The aborigines gave the Devil's Gorge area a wide berth, calling it a place of strong magic. Others picked up on the abnormal atmosphere, too. But the cattle didn't seem to mind; there were times, like now, when they gathered in large numbers and had to be chased out. It was a ground job for two rounds of the mustering team and not one for the helicopter. Helicopters cost money. Besides, the cattle were getting so smart they'd begun to realize that though the chopper made a lot of noise and hovered menacingly above them, it couldn't actually touch them.

Mustering cattle was dangerous work, requiring courage, skill and quite a bit of fancy riding. At one stage, a great red kangaroo leapt out stupidly, roo-fashion, in Rachael Munro's path, causing her mare to prop so violently Rachael would have shot over its head were it not for her strong young wrists and lightning reflexes. As it was, her arms felt as though they'd been pulled out of their sockets, her cotton shirt was stuck to the hollow of her back, and her vision was blurred from all the sweat that had run into her eyes.

Rachael pulled off her battered akubra and began to fan herself with it, a useless gesture in the parched air. The elastic band that secured her thick plait, weakened by so much moisture, suddenly snapped, sending her hair cascading down her back. Wonderful hair. A rich, curling, dark red. Not that Rachael spent much time on its grooming. There were more important things to do. When she had a chance she'd have it cut short. For now, it could stay in its easy-care braid.

She smoothed the heavy mass over one shoulder, while wisping curls sprang out around her temples and cheeks. She had a crick in her neck from always glancing back at the men or the cattle, and she began to rub it, turning her head gingerly this way and that. Her usual vital energy, so much a part of her, was at a perilously low level. She was working too hard, driving herself through the days in a vain effort to cope with her grief. Early morning was the worst, bringing with it the waking realization that she would never see her father again. Survival, she'd been told by many kind people, lay in keeping on the go. It helped, but not much. She desperately wanted to regress to the time when her father was alive.

Thirty feet away, a log suddenly stood up on powerful squat legs and pounded away across the scorched earth. *That* brought her back to the present and her heart gave a momentary quake. A goanna, fully six feet long—a perfect monster. No matter how many times she saw one, and she'd lived with them all her life, they always managed to give her a fright. And why not? A few years back, one of them had clambered up a mounted stockman mistaking him for a tree, and the hapless man had to be treated for shock and bad lacerations by the Royal Flying Doctor. A day later, out fencing, he had suffered a mild heart attack, but he'd survived to laugh about it and grow blasé about the savage charms of the bush.

As Rachael rested, a flight of sulfur-crested white cockatoos wheeled over the camp in a V formation, then came down to rest in the branches of the kurrajongs, completely without fear of the men beneath. It was a cheering sight, and it made Rachael's brilliant blue eyes mist over with the sudden tears she spent a lot of time these days blinking away. She loved the birds, the millions of them that filled the infinite blue-and-gold air of the outback. The great wedge-tailed eagles, the falcons and hawks, parrots, rosellas, white and black cockatoos, corellas, the rose-pink galahs, orange and crimson chats, finch and quail, the legions of pelicans and the vast flights of budgerigar. Nature was the great healer. It lifted the desolation.

The billy had boiled and the men were drinking their tea, ribbing one another in a tired, desultory fashion. Matt Pritchard, Miriwin's foreman and Rachael's best mate from early childhood, limped toward her carrying two fragrant mugs. A big, powerful, good-humored man of fifty-six, he looked dusty, aching and characteristically stoic. His leg was obviously playing up, legacy of an encounter with a vicious scrub bull, and Rachael commented on it solicitously.

Matt broke into a comical little dance, cut abruptly short. "Not to worry, love. I've learned to live with it. It's been under a bit of pressure today. Here, take your mug before I spill the lot."

Rachael reached up thankfully and Matt sat down beside her, slapping at a few flies that sluggishly droned away. "After you finish it, I want you to go back to the house. It's only going to get harder and you've done quite enough."

"I'll feel better after the break."

Matt held up a sun-mottled hand. "No arguments now. They won't work. I've got your best interests at heart. That being so, I have to call a stop. Since your dad passed on, you've been pushing yourself to the limit. I can understand why—but the boys are getting worried about you. This can't go on."

"So what do you want me to do—take to my bed?"

"That'll be the day!" Matt flashed her a wry grin. "But you don't have to hurl yourself into backbreaking work, either. I know how you feel, love. I know your feelings go deep. But I can't allow it to go on. I've been lookin' out for you since you were a little nipper climbing a fence so you could get onto a horse, and I'm not going to stop now. The more so since your dad's gone and no one else seems to care."

"You make it sound pretty depressing."

"It *is* depressing." Matt shook his head with real anger. "I'd have a few words with your stepmother, only she'd try to fire me, and that wouldn't help anyone, least of all you. I get the impression she doesn't give a damn about you anymore. She doesn't even notice you're gettin' downright scrawny."

"Hang on a minute. *Scrawny?*" Rachael looked at him with a challenging light in her eyes.

"You know. Delicate, fragile. A real damn problem."

"So I've lost weight?" Rachael shrugged. "It doesn't interfere with doing my work, Matt."

He gazed at his legs stretched out in front of him. "No one's denying your fighting spirit, Rae. Or your ability to do the job. But it all seems rather pointless if you're going to kill yourself. There's no sense to it. You're a beautiful young lady, twenty-three years old. You should be enjoying yourself."

"Wild parties. Booze. Boyfriends?" Rachael teased him.

"Parties and boyfriends wouldn't be out of place. I figure it's time you had a bit of fun. That brother of yours knows how to enjoy himself."

"Scotty has a different attitude to life," Rachael said with a dry edge to her voice.

"You can say that again!" Matt snorted in disgust. "*You* should've been the boy, the son. It's really crazy how it goes sometimes. I hate to say it, but your stepmother turned Scotty into one spoiled rotten kid. Why, he couldn't even stay a day after the funeral!"

Rachael remembered very clearly, but she pushed all the hurt to the back of her mind. "He was upset, Matt. He didn't know how to handle the situation."

"All he had to do was be supportive. You'd think it would come naturally."

"Scotty's a bit like Sonia. They don't like the bad times." She shrugged again. "It's human, Matt."

Matt nodded and shoved his empty mug to one side. "It's a good thing you're so brave. I don't think I'm being too hard on the boy, Rae. The time's right for him to assume some responsibility, not leave it all to his sister."

"Absolutely!" Rachael agreed. "He's going to be a great help in the office."

"If you can get him there." Matt wouldn't be cajoled. He kicked at the ground with the heel of his riding boot. "You want to take a look at the way you spoil him, too, Rae. That boy needs toughening up. Your father loved you, but he was darn strict with you. You always had to toe the line, while Scotty ran wild like a brumby. It don't make no sense—and in most things your dad was a real sensible man."

"Scotty was the apple of his eye, Matt. He could do no wrong. Some men are like that about their sons."

Matt shook his head sadly. "Darlin' girl, you know as well as I do, the boy's not cut out for station life. You either love it or you hate it. No in-betweens. Your dad faced most things, yet he wouldn't face that."

"Scotty might still come to it, Matt," Rachael argued. "He needs time. He's so *young.*"

"And you're so much older?" Matt snorted. "You get nothin' for yourself, Rae. No one spoils *you* or ever has, yet you're worth ten of your brother."

Rachael leaned sideways and kissed Matt's dusty cheek. "You're as biased as they come and aren't I glad of it! You've always been there for me, Matt. You and Wyn. You're more family than the family I have left. Maybe Dad didn't love me the way he loved Scott, but he *did* love me."

"Of course he did," Matt said quickly. "Of course he did, Rae."

"It's not uncommon for men to favor their sons over their daughters. I should have known Scott would inherit control of Miriwin."

"Sixty percent with you and your stepma sharing the rest. It's not fair." Matt made a face.

"Maybe not. But the fact that I'm a female was the deciding factor with Dad. He always said I'd go off and get married. He didn't want Miriwin falling into another family's hands. You can understand that."

"It's not as straightforward as that," Matt said morosely. "Instead of holding on to it, Scotty and your stepmother will probably sell it out from under you."

The thought was so shocking the mug shook in Rachael's hand. "What are you saying, Matt?" She turned a blind face to him.

"It has to be faced, girl."

"Scotty *wouldn't* sell out, Matt. He *loves* being a Munro of Miriwin Station and all that goes with it."

"You mean he's a snob like your stepmother." Matt slapped his huge palms together, obviously upset.

"Doesn't that mean he *wouldn't* sell? We mightn't be up there with the Carradines, but the Munros are a minor dynasty. God knows Scotty's always lived like a lord. Dad idolized him, and Sonia thinks he can do no wrong."

"More's the pity! I never saw a boy so spoiled and self-indulgent. I don't have a whole lot of sympathy for him. Especially since the funeral."

"I understand, Matt, but I love him. Nothing can change that."

Matt's leg was obviously punishing him and he grimaced in pain. "I know you love him, Rae, and he loves you. That's the only thing that saves him as far as I'm concerned. It doesn't mean, however, he won't let you down."

There were shadows of exhaustion beneath Rachael's eyes. "He *can't*, Matt. Munros have worked Miriwin for more than 120 years. That's a long time in this part of the world."

Matt took out his handkerchief and blew his nose violently. "Heritage is important to you, Rae, not to Scott. And don't forget your stepma. She always worked on your dad about Scotty's inheriting, but I'm willing to bet if the price is right she'd encourage him to sell. All she was ever interested in was the money. She'd have big bucks, instead of this drought-stricken land. Rumor has it—and it's only rumor, mind—that Curt Carradine might be interested in Miriwin if it ever came on the market."

Rachael was so devastated she visibly paled. "Say that again, Matt?"

"Now don't get het up," he cautioned. "Talkin' to you about Curt these days is like throwing a match into a pile of dry leaves." He paused. "You know the old stories, Rae, though I guess a lot of them are long buried. Curt's grandfather was always after this property, and his father before him. There were big tensions between the Carradines and Munros over the issue. It was Curt's dad who brought you all back together. A fine man, not ruthless like the Old Man or brilliant like Curt, but a peacemaker and well-respected. But even he made no bones about the fact that he considered Miriwin a highly desirable property. It stands on Carrara's border, and we have a good deep stretch of the river. Liquid gold in the drought. Curt would be a fool not to snaffle it up if it ever came on the market, and a fool he ain't."

"Wouldn't it bother him to push us off our land?" Rachael asked, her voice intense. "Miriwin isn't what it was, and he's got enough already. A whole hunk of the country. Landsdown cost him ten million. He must have his own mint."

Matt turned to her with wry humor in his eyes. "I figure he has, too. Curt's the smartest operator we've seen since the days of the old cattle kings. Increasing the empire is just part of his job."

"Where did you get this rumor from, Matt?" Rachael asked.

"Three or four sources, as it happens. Ray Henderson's one."

"That old bore!"

"And a mine of information. Reckon he picked it up on a Carradine outstation. 'Course, there's been talk since your dad died. No one much liked the way the will went, and your stepma has never bothered about earning the outback's goodwill. Women in her position are generally tireless workers for good causes, but she never did take an interest. A city woman she was and a city woman she remains. I wouldn't put it past her to sound Curt out."

"They've certainly grown close enough," Rachael said bleakly. "This is a revelation to me, Matt. I think I'd *hate* Curt if he ever came after us."

"Now that's just plain silly, Rae." Matt shook her arm. "Curt's no raider. He's an honorable man. All I'm sayin' is he'd listen if anyone was talkin'. Surely you can see the sense in that. Why, I remember a time you had quite a crush on him."

Rachael shook her head.

"Adolescent craziness."

"Look at it this way. If Scott and your stepmother put Miriwin on the market, someone would buy it. Why not Curt? He'd restore it to its old glory, if anyone would."

Rachael looked at him in astonishment. "You're talking like this is a foregone conclusion, Matt. No one's said anything to me. I *do* have a twenty-percent share. I'd consider it unethical if Sonia and Curt were having discussions behind my back."

Matt shifted uneasily. "I'm certain Curt wouldn't do it that way. If there was any *real* talk, I mean. Besides, your stepma has a lot of influence with Scotty, but she'd still have to wait until he got home."

"Sonia's always had a soft spot for Curt," Rachael said bluntly. "Maybe she's going to offer him a package. *Her* and the station. I think she'd do it for sure if she were younger."

"Well, she's not exactly old," Matt pointed out dryly. "A damned good-lookin' woman, if you like porcelain dolls." Matt twisted his aching leg this way and that. "I'm sorry if I've upset you, Rae, but I'm bound to put you in the picture as I see it."

"Why haven't I known, Matt?" Rachael asked with intense disgust. "Why haven't I been more *suspicious?*"

"Don't blame Curt here," Matt warned. "I think you might be makin' the biggest mistake of your life. He was a very good friend to your dad. When he had his bad breaks, Curt helped him out. He's been right neighborly since your dad died. Your stepma has come to lean on him."

"And I resent that like hell." Rachael's blue eyes flashed.

"Why, Rae?" Matt asked quietly.

A blush reddened her cheeks. "I'm thinking of Dad. Sonia's pursuing Curt Carradine, and Dad's hardly buried. I don't know, it seems so disloyal. Not only that, I suspect she's mistaking Curt's interest in her...." Rachael's voice trailed off.

"Your stepma can take care of herself," Matt said sardonically. "I can give you that in writing."

Rachael picked up a twig and began to draw aimlessly in the sand. "I miss Dad terribly, Matt."

"Sure you do." Matt gave her an affectionate glance.

"It's an empty house without him."

Matt, a sensitive man beneath the granite exterior, patted her shoulder. "Your dad was a good man taken before his time. A freak accident! Even now I can't believe it."

"It was too sudden, Matt. Too violent. He was here in the morning. Gone by night."

Minutes passed while they looked sightlessly at the burned ground. Alex Munro had been working a tractor, pulling out an old tree stump, when the tractor had rolled, fatally crushing him.

"You see why I don't want to give it up, Matt. We'll hold on to this land. It's what Dad wanted. What he expected."

Matt sighed. "Wanting doesn't always make it happen," he said finally. "We'll continue to do our best. There's always the drought to punish us. I can't think when we had the last drop of rain. Look at that sky!"

"Like the hot blue of a peacock's wing." Rachael, the nature lover, murmured. "Glittering. Cloudless. Do you suppose Dad's up there on the other side?"

"I just bet he is!" Matt said comfortingly. He got to his feet and held out his hand. "Go home now, love. I can hold the fort. I've been doing it long enough."

"That you have, Matt," Rachael acknowledged, her resistance gone. "I can't think what we'd do without you."

"Tell that to your stepma." Matt grinned. "She always acts like the sight of me offends her."

"You don't bow and scrape enough, Matt," Rachael said, dusting herself off.

"I've got too much pride," Matt told her. "Just like you...."

AT THE CREEK Rachael dismounted, allowing the mare to drink loudly and thirstily of the sluggish brown water. It would do her no harm. In the good times the creek was a place of great beauty. Heavily scented by the native boronia, the water ran deep and sweet. The transparent green was shot through with spears of gold where the sun penetrated the thick canopy of coolabahs and bauhinias, trees that were startlingly beautiful when in flower. Now it was little more than a series of water holes in a wide, sandy bed, the grasses lining its edge stunted and as yellow as spinifex.

One more burning ridge before home.

Home? Rachael bit down on the pain. She knew now beyond any doubt that only her father had held them together. It'd been six months since the accident—no time at all, yet more than enough to show Rachael that Sonia had little real feeling for her. She was another woman's child and always had been. Whatever bond had existed between her and Sonia had broken entirely at her father's death. Tragedy had not drawn them together; Sonia had no need of her company or comfort. Rachael and Scotty remained close, though Rachael was forced to acknowledge that Scotty wanted nothing to do with the running of Miriwin. Not, at any rate, for the time being. Their father had always claimed Scotty would become more responsible with maturity. Well, his chance had come. If Curt Carradine wanted Miriwin, God help them all.

Now that the issue had been raised, Rachael began to recall the old stories Matt had mentioned. If they were true, Curt's great-grandfather had all but resorted to force to annex Miriwin. There was one shocking incident when the two men, Carradine and Munro, had confronted each other with guns. Curt's father had indeed brought peace. The whole outback mourned when he lost his life in a light-plane crash in King's Canyon eight years before. Curt's mother, devastated at her loss, had packed up and left the station, never to return. The sins of the forefathers had visited tragedy on both houses.

At the top of the ridge Rachael looked down on Miriwin homestead and its satellite buildings. There was no point in denying that she suddenly felt terribly threatened. Could the past rise again? Miriwin was a fine house of which anyone would be proud. Double storied with wide, deep verandas, it had a central core constructed of hand-cut freestone quarried on the property, and all the woodwork and the splendid staircase were of cedar. In her grandfather's day, it had been famous for merino sheep and cattle. But gradually the sheep that had earned the family fortune had been phased out as the wool industry fought for survival.

The view from the ridge was superb. Miriwin homestead stood romantically shrouded by its trees, the meandering gardens kept green by artesian water. The whole scene vibrated in the ever-present mirage. How she loved it! Rachael was like the Munros before her—Miriwin was everything to her, a way of life she never wanted to change. The spirit of the outback had been part of her since birth. Not Scotty, though. To Scott, Miriwin was a glamorous weekender. He always came with a changing circle of friends. Dancing in the old ballroom. Plenty of food and drink. The magnificent swimming pool their father had put in for him. Fine horses to ride around the property, its area diminished over the years as the family was overtaken by a series of financial setbacks, but still impressive to Scotty's friends. Once, in her grandfather's day, the hospitality on Miriwin had been legendary, but that had fallen off as the station suffered reversals.

By the time she reached the stables, Rachael was ready to fall into a hot tub and soak. She handed over the mare to Jacky Eaglehawk, a young aboriginal boy, invaluable with the horses, then made her way up to the house. Normally she would have entered through Wyn's kitchen, but for some reason she walked to the front of the house, noticing sections of wrought iron on the upper balcony were in sad need of repair.

The sound of voices on the veranda halted her. Or rather *a* voice. The sort of voice that sent shivers shooting down a woman's spine. *Talk of the devil and he turns up on your doorstep.* If they hadn't been working Devil's Gorge she would have seen the Cessna fly in. Rachael glanced down at her sweat-soaked shirt and dusty jeans. The left leg of her jeans had a spectacular rent in it, courtesy of a particularly rough ride.

It was an unhappy fact of life that she never looked her best when she needed her confidence. She had to backtrack as fast as she could.

It was too late. Sonia called to her in her soft, husky tones. "Rachael, is that you out there?" The question seemed to require no response, for Sonia went on, "Don't run away. Come up and see who's here."

Rachael closed her eyes, mortified. She was trapped. *Come up and see who's here?* she thought ruefully. As if she didn't know. An endless stream of people had visited in the past months, but no one sounded remotely like Curt Carradine. That voice of his was midway between a dark rasp and a honeyed smoothness, crackling with authority. Rachael had seen its effect on women. Including Sonia. Today she decided to take offense on behalf of the family. When had Sonia given up mourning?

Rachael marched up the steps, staring at the man who returned her sparkling gaze calmly. John Curtis Carradine at the family's service. She'd known him all her life and for years turned every color of the rainbow whenever he spoke to her. Worse, he seemed to watch for it. His status was so exalted, his family and its history so much the history of landed Australia, that just to be singled out was a great honor. So why did he generate so many complex emotions in her these days? When all was said and done, she worshiped him like everyone else. But there was no getting away from the fact that it irked her to see him and Sonia drawing so close. As she'd told Matt, it seemed so disloyal to her father's memory.

Curt, the privileged aristocrat, came to his feet, a rangy six foot three. To say he was handsome didn't say it at all. He was much more than that. He was *electrifying*. Tough, dynamic, blazing with the sort of energy that flared out and caught you. No woman could take him in at one glance, but Rachael tried.

Today he wore everyday gear—a khaki bush shirt, moleskins, glossy boots on his feet—yet he managed to make it look the ultimate form of dress. A wide fancy belt was slung around his lean waist. A cream akubra with a snake band lay on the chair beside him. In appearance and personality, no ordinary man. A man who'd had enormous responsibility thrust on him, too young. In his own way he was an outback prince.

Sonia was sitting back in the peacock chair, fanning herself. Her apple-blossom skin, religiously shielded from the sun, was uncharacteristically flushed. Her pale blue eyes were glassy with excitement. She looked extraordinarily youthful and pretty, and now Rachael came to think of it, like a kitten with a bowl of cream.

"Take your hat off, dear," she begged Rachael in silky tones. "I hate the way you cram it down on your head. It's *so* unfeminine."

"Better than getting badly sunburned." Rachael removed her hat and spun it with unerring aim to land on the high finial of a wicker chair. Satisfied, she walked toward Curt, holding out her fine-boned, callused hand. "How are you, Curt?" she asked crisply, her eyes bright with hostility. "It's always a pleasure to see you at Miriwin." How was *that* for a straight shot?

It appeared to amuse, not wound.

"From the blaze in your eyes I would have thought my welcome was wearing out," he drawled.

Despite herself, she swallowed. "No, it's still holding." He had the most extraordinary eyes. On occasion, pure gold. They reminded Rachael of a lion's. Splendid and scary at the same time.

"So what have you been doing to look so exhausted?" he asked in the big-brother tones he seemed to reserve for her.

"I'm on my feet, aren't I?"

"You may be on your feet, but they won't hold you up much longer. You're swaying. Here, sit down." He pulled out a chair and without thinking Rachael slid down in it.

Her whole body was aching and she did have a tremble in her legs. Trust him to notice.

"She's been mustering, Curt," Sonia explained in troubled tones. "It's impossible to stop her. Whenever I try, she makes such a fuss."

"When is that, Sonia? It seems to me I'm gone before you're out of bed." Rachael glanced at her stepmother challengingly, but Sonia's eyes were unresponsive, unblinking.

"It's not necessary for you to do a stockman's work, Rachael."

Rachael shrugged. "I've got to spend my time somehow. One of these days it might rain. We'll want the mustering done."

"So where were you?" Curt persisted.

"Devil's Gorge."

His black, peaked brows drew together. "That's rough country, Rachael. I'm surprised Matt let you go along."

"I can handle it," Rachael said shortly.

His handsome mouth thinned. "I guess you can, if you don't give a damn about life and limb."

"I'm not a child, Curt." Rachael felt heat rise in her cheeks. "You always treat me like one. I'm twenty-three, you know."

"Well, I thank you for reminding me."

"You've very willful." Sonia sided with Curt. "If anything happens I'll hold Matt responsible. He allows you far too much freedom."

"I figure I'm the boss," Rachael said laconically. "Anyway, Matt sent me home." One side of her hair tumbled forward and she swept it back in irritation.

"Was Matt using the chopper?" Curt asked.

"Too expensive. Besides, the cattle are so damned smart they know they're safe if they stay put."

Curt eased back to lean against the balustrade, arms spread on either side. "A good chopper pilot can cope with just about any situation. You can't put too much pressure on cattle. That's when they refuse to budge." It was Sonia he addressed. "I'd like to have a word with Matt, if you don't mind, Sonia. I have a good chopper pilot working for me at the moment. I could spare him for a few hours."

Sonia looked at him with wide-eyed gratitude. "You're so *good* to us, Curt."

Rachael couldn't take it. "Thanks, Curt, but that won't be necessary. We're managing." The longer they stayed obliged to him, the worse it would get.

"I expect *Matt* will be glad of help," he countered, neatly putting her in her place. "I'll check with him later."

"He won't be in until sundown." Rachael was unable to keep the satisfaction out of her voice. "You'll be long gone by then."

"On the contrary, Rachael," Sonia intervened sharply. "I've asked Curt to stay overnight. He's been extremely good to us these last terrible months. So would you please get down off your very high horse?"

"I'll do one better." Rachael swooped to her feet and to her consternation found herself reeling. "I'll go soak my head."

"Steady!" Curt moved like lightning, catching her by the shoulder. "You're all right, aren't you?"

She glanced up briefly into his eyes. "Yes."

"You're a stubborn little beggar," he muttered softly.

"I'm a Munro, Curt. A Munro of Miriwin. Remember it."

RACHAEL HAD BEEN in her bedroom barely ten minutes when Sonia burst in, looking flushed and cross. "Where are your manners, Rachael? Every time Curt comes over these days it's like undeclared war.''

"That's a bit of an exaggeration, isn't it?"

"I don't think so. Do you think he doesn't feel your aggression? It's not exactly hidden."

"What's he doing here all the time, Sonia?" Rachael asked bluntly.

Her stepmother's blue gaze went chilly. "Might I remind you *I* am mistress of this house?"

"Put a sock in it, Sonia," Rachael said tiredly. "This is my home, too. As far as that goes, Dad left us on pretty much of an equal footing."

Sonia seemed genuinely affronted. "Why, you ungrateful little wretch! I think I deserve more respect. All these years I've raised you—and how have you repaid me?"

"By giving you no trouble at all. Scotty was always the one to play up. I had to toe the line, while you and Dad spoiled Scotty rotten."

"My dear, you're jealous." Sonia laughed.

Rachael started to unbutton her blouse, hoping Sonia would leave so she could slip into the bath. "You want complete honesty, Sonia? There's nothing about Scotty to be jealous of. At the moment he hasn't got a single thought in his head outside enjoying himself."

"He's preparing for his final exams," Sonia snapped, obviously on the brink of a confrontation. "You *are* jealous of your stepbrother, Rachael. Your father never even glanced at you when Scotty was around."

"That's a cruel thing to say, Sonia, and it's not true," Rachael said, trying to push away the pain.

"Of course it is." Sonia moved into a velvet upholstered armchair. "Scotty was the light of his life. He proved it by leaving him control of Miriwin."

"Even Dad made mistakes." Rachael found herself retaliating. "He had two kids, but only one of them finished up with the lot. I'm not overjoyed about it, but I won't fight it. Not while Miriwin stays in the family."

"I don't follow you." Sonia frowned.

"Forget it," Rachael begged. "I'm tired and dusty and covered in sweat."

"And don't you like to stress that in front of Curt!"

"Meaning what?"

"I have to wonder, for all your little resentments, if you're over your crush?" Sonia said archly.

"I'll answer that with a great big *yes*. I'm not after Curt Carradine's attention or sympathy. I know he's being a big help to us, Sonia, but I'm beginning to question his motives."

The cucumber-cool Sonia blushed scarlet. "Curt Carradine helps everyone!"

Rachael walked to a chest of drawers and took out fresh underwear. "I respect that, Sonia, but we see far more of him than we used to."

"Is it so extraordinary he might want to see *me*?" Sonia demanded.

All Rachael's worst fears, the nameless anxieties, came together. "What do you mean?" she asked finally.

Sonia hugged her slender arms around her body. "Don't look at me with such dismay in your eyes. I'm thirty-nine years old. Still young enough for a man to look at me."

Rachael sank onto the sofa, while the remaining strength ebbed from her body. "Of course you are, Sonia, but you can't mean *Curt!*"

"Now you're being cruel." Fretfully Sonia twisted the gold wedding band and the magnificent solitaire diamond she wore on her left hand. "I've always been regarded as a good-looking woman."

"You are, Sonia," Rachael agreed. "But what about Dad? We've only just lost him."

"I can't allow it to destroy me, Rachael," Sonia said passionately. "I miss your father terribly, but he's *gone.* That's what you can't seem to get into your head. I must have a man in my life. I *must* remarry. Curt's a few years younger, true, but he has such...maturity. And society is getting used to men marrying older women. Especially women who have so much to offer."

"Sonia, you could get badly hurt."

"Thank you, Rachael," Sonia responded bitterly. "Maybe your shock has something to do with your own feelings for Curt. But face it. He thinks of you as a child. He's watched you grow up. And lately, while you've been busy trying to avoid him, Curt and I have grown closer. We always did have an excellent rapport."

"You're pretty vulnerable right now, Sonia. You're putting yourself a little too much into Curt's hands. Don't forget, he can have any woman he wants. The polo set idolize him. Andrée Haddon has been hanging in there for years."

Sonia cast Rachael a pitying glance. "Andrée is very attractive and she comes from the right kind of family, but she's no match for me. I can hold my own with the best of them. I'm a sophisticated woman and I do have a lot to offer. I'm even young enough to have more children."

Rachael held her head in both hands in an effort to contain herself. "Sonia, you've only recently been widowed. Grief takes people in unaccountable ways. You must allow yourself more time."

"That's the very thing I *can't* do," Sonia replied.

"Do you suppose Curt knows what's on your mind?" Rachael demanded. "If so, I'm going to go downstairs and kick him out."

"Oh, don't be such a fool, Rachael," Sonia said shortly. "I know exactly how to behave. When your father first visited my parents' home twenty years ago, he had no thought of marrying me. I was the youngest daughter of the house, scarcely out of college. Even then I knew what I wanted. I wanted to be Mrs. Alexander Munro of Miriwin Station. I'm thankful for twenty good years. It takes nothing from your father that I want to remarry."

"After six months?" Rachael asked incredulously.

"Of course not after six months. But, say, a year. I think Curt might enjoy taking care of me full-time."

"Dad left you enough money to take care of yourself."

"You don't understand anything, do you?" Sonia asked with brooding intensity. "You don't know how women like me feel."

Rachael bit hard on her lip. "Lord, Sonia, I have a fair idea. So you've always fancied Curt in a...respectable way? It would be fatal to fall in love with him."

"How do you stop it from happening?" Sonia shrugged.

"A holiday. You can go to your friends in Sydney again. You never had any trouble taking off in the past. Dad always gave you plenty of freedom."

"My dear, he knew he had to," Sonia said, narrowing her eyes. "I was a good wife to your father, Rachael. I gave him a son. It wasn't my fault the marriage wasn't a big success."

Rachael lifted her hand. "Please don't say any more, Sonia. It's private. Between you and Dad."

"Your father was a good man, but he was years older than me. He wasn't very... affectionate."

"Maybe you had something to do with that," Rachael countered. "Don't put all the blame on Dad. Are you aware Curt might have plans for taking over Miriwin?" she asked in an abrupt change of subject.

Sonia blinked slowly, her blue eyes opaque. "Wherever did you get that?"

"A rumor that's circulating."

"Rumors. The air's thick with them!" Sonia laughed. "Don't think I don't know what people think of me. I've never fitted in."

"You've never tried."

"Thank you, Rachael," Sonia replied sarcastically. "I'm not a do-gooder, never was. I loathe women's committees and all that. At the same time, we've always given sizable donations to this cause and that. *You're* the one everyone loves. A splendid country woman. Too horsey for my taste."

Rachael ignored her stepmother's little barb, long used to them. "So you haven't heard any of this from Curt?" she persisted.

"That would upset you, wouldn't it?" Sonia jeered. "The Carradines have always been interested in Miriwin. You know that."

"Sonia, can I get a direct answer?" Rachael pleaded.

Sonia made an irritable movement. "Curt hasn't said any such thing," she told Rachael sharply. "You are so tiresome on the subject of Miriwin. It's not as though you had a lot at stake. Scott has the controlling interest. Scott and I don't share your mad obsession with the land. It's crazy! We're right in the middle of a drought."

"The drought will break, Sonia, if we just hold on."

"Hold on?" Sonia all but shouted. "What the hell for? You're just like your father. I had to live with that obsession for years. The land is more important than anything else!"

"The land abides, Sonia. It's here when we've gone."

"Well, I'm still here and I'm more interested in the here and now," Sonia said. "You really should have been a boy, Rachael. I quite see that."

"I don't have to be a man to run Miriwin."

"Except that your father left it to Scott."

"You did tell him Scott would grow into the job."

Sonia looked at her stepdaughter with cynical eyes. "Would a mother do anything else? You surely didn't think I'd nominate you for the job. When all's said and done, Rachael, you're not my own flesh and blood. Scotty is."

"Do you have *any* feeling for me?" Rachael asked suddenly. "Things have been so strained between us since we lost Dad."

"You're a woman now, Rachael," Sonia said, giving Rachael a jaded look. "There's always friction when two women live under the same roof. Of course I'm fond of you, but we rub one another the wrong way. It's not anything either of us can help."

"Do you want me to go?" Rachael asked wryly.

Sonia's small, regular features tightened. "As you've been good enough to point out, Rachael, I can't tell you what to do. I haven't the slightest doubt the situation will resolve itself in time. It may be an old-fashioned view, but if you ever decide to do anything about yourself, you could make a good marriage. You have lots of assets, yet you insist on doing nothing with them."

"I'd look damned silly dressed up for the cows," Rachael commented.

Sonia, on the other hand, was always impeccably groomed. She sat in the armchair looking sensational. Her blue silk shirt matched her eyes. Her white linen slacks were beautifully cut. Stylish pewter sandals adorned her small, narrow feet, matching the glimmer of her silver earrings and bangles. Her fine, silky blond hair was always kept short in the latest style, giving her a very youthful appearance. Nearly forty, she'd never looked more attractive. The trauma of recent months didn't show on her face at all. In fact, it was becoming increasingly obvious that Sonia felt she'd mourned long enough.

Now she stood up, smoothing the creases of her slacks. "Curt and I won't mind if you're too tired to join us for dinner."

"I refuse to sit in my room," Rachael answered.

"In that case, wear something decent and try to remember that Curt is an honoured guest."

Rachael didn't respond.

"Another thing." Sonia paused at the door. "Don't try to make difficulties between Curt and me. I think you'd like to, given the chance."

Despite herself Rachael laughed. "You're wrong about that, Sonia. You're a free agent. I realize that now. But not when it comes to Miriwin. This is my home. This is where I was born. This is where I hope to die. I have one request. Don't go having discussions with Curt Carradine without telling me."

"Is that some kind of a threat, Rachael?" Sonia asked, raising a supercilious brow.

"Not a threat. A request for consideration. So far as I'm concerned, no Carradine will get Miriwin. Except over my dead body."

CHAPTER TWO

AN HOUR LATER, Rachael was lying on her back staring up at the ornately plastered ceiling of her bedroom. Wyn, Matt's wife and Miriwin's longtime housekeeper, popped her head around the door.

"Not disturbing you, am I, love?"

"Of course not, Wyn, come in." Rachael sat up, her hands clasped loosely in her lap. "I've just been lying here trying to figure out what's going on."

"You and me both!" Wyn, plump, pleasant-looking, with fresh unlined skin and a bubble of short gray curls, headed for a chair and fell unceremoniously into it. "I can only stay a minute. Such shenanigans when Mr. Carradine comes to visit. The Limoges dinner set tonight. I expect you've never even seen it. A group of little silver candlesticks, instead of the candelabra. Porcelain ornaments. Talk about ostentatious! But it seems important to your stepmother. You dad used to like a simple setting. Anyway, love, you were saying?"

"I feel as though a bomb's been dropped on me. I have to know—what's Curt doing here all the time?"

Wyn laughed abruptly. Not her usual infectious chuckle, but one with some irony. "Maybe your stepmother thinks it's to see her."

Rachael reached out and gripped a pillow fiercely. "Could that be possible, Wyn?"

"It's probably more in your stepmother's mind," the woman responded.

Rachael shook back her long curly hair, her expression upset. "I can't believe this is happening. We only lost Dad a few months ago."

"That's true," Wyn sighed, "but there's no use being judgmental, love. You have to realize everyone's different now."

"But Curt and Sonia? He's *years* younger than she is, Wyn. He can have anyone he wants."

Wyn nodded. "Your stepmother probably calls *him,* I shouldn't wonder. Asks for advice. Acts helpless."

"She *has* come to lean on him," Rachael agreed. "Matt warned me today there's been some talk Curt might be interested in Miriwin if it ever came on the market."

"Matt did? The old devil, he didn't tell me. I suppose it could be true, love. The issue goes back a long way. But I can't think Curt Carradine would conspire to push you off your property. Still, it's possible your stepmother could have said something to him."

"She denies it," Rachael said. "She has no right to discuss it with him, Wyn. Miriwin isn't hers to sell."

Wyn's expression was rueful. "Darling girl, I don't want to upset you, but you've often said it yourself. Neither Scotty nor your stepma share your feeling for Miriwin."

"They haven't even straightened out Dad's affairs," Rachael said bitterly.

"They will in time."

There was a silence while Rachael considered. "I think the two of them—Sonia and Curt—are up to something."

Wyn shook her head so emphatically her curls bounced. "Not Curt. He's straight as an arrow, inside and out."

"If that's the case, why is he here so often? What are they talking about?"

"If you want my opinion, he's keeping an eye on you."

"What?" Rachael sat bolt upright. "God love you, Wyn, but you're wrong about that."

"I wouldn't be too sure, love. Curt's known you all your life. It's only to be expected he'd want to look out for you. Someone has to. These last months, it's like your stepmother doesn't care for you at all."

Rachael stared down at the silk brocade bedspread. "She reminded me I'm not her flesh and blood. I think it really hit her when Dad died. At any rate I seem to put her out of sorts."

"She feels the same way about the rest of us," Wyn muttered in a dry voice. "None of us has ever won her over. But it's you I'm worried about. Matt tells me your grief is making you reckless."

"Oh, nonsense, Wyn." Rachael shrugged that off. "Matt's like an old hen with a chick."

"Be that as it may, he's worried about you, Rae. We've looked after you for most of your life. We love you like our own. I know you're missing your daddy terribly. You've never had a proper relationship with your stepmother and you're driving yourself too hard. Matt said you're taking risks. The boys are worried, as well. They've all got the same idea. To protect you."

"They want me to stop working?"

"They don't want you to stop doing what you love, but it has to be safe. Matt tried to put you off the muster."

"I'm as good as any of the boys," Rachael declared.

"No one's saying you're not capable, Rae. You're full of spunk, but you're hurtin'. We can all see that. You hurt. We hurt. Can you imagine how we'd all feel if there was another accident? Accidents are more likely when your mind's fazed and you're not eating right."

"I'm trying to cope, Wyn, the best way I can." It was a cry from the heart, and Wyn responded with deep understanding and love.

"I know, dear, but it might be as well to rest up a bit. Your stepmother had a holiday with those smart friends of hers in Sydney. Scotty hasn't been back since the funeral. It might be a good idea if you went away for a holiday, too. I was having a little chat with Mr. Carradine, and he said the same thing."

"I just bet he'd like me out of the way."

Wyn tilted her head back and stared at the ceiling. "Listen, don't go getting mad on the basis of a rumor. That man has your best interests at heart."

"Your bias is showing, Wyn."

"He's absolutely wonderful," Wyn maintained stoutly.

"You're in love with him," Rachael teased. "Like all the rest."

"I don't see that's doing anyone any harm," Wyn said with a laugh.

"If he ever tries taking Miriwin from us, he'll have an enemy for life," Rachael said, abruptly sobering.

"Even if he's the best person to take it over?" Wyn asked. "Let's face it, if Miriwin came on the market and Curt didn't acquire it, someone else would. Would you hate that person, too?"

"You bet!"

Wyn groaned and got to her feet. "What are you going to do with your hair tonight, love?"

"Looks terrible, does it?" Rachael lifted a careless hand and swatted at the thick, curling masses. "It's always impossible when I wash it."

"It's glorious hair!" Wyn confirmed proudly. "But it does have a tendency to run riot. I'll tell you what. I'll pop back later and do it in a roll. The style doesn't suit everyone but it looks lovely on you." She walked to the wardrobe and peered in. "Glory, don't you need some clothes! Your stepma has more outfits than Princess Di."

"And more shoes than Princess Di and Imelda Marcos put together. Dad didn't deny her anything."

"The little lady knew how to get to him. Now, what about this?" Wyn held Rachael's best dress to her plump figure.

Rachael laughed. "You're assuming, *hoping,* Curt's going to spend some time looking at me?"

"He's a man, isn't he?" Wyn flashed back. "When I tell you you're beautiful, you don't believe me. Maybe that's another little thing that's putting your stepma's nose out of joint."

"What, little ol' me from the backwoods?" She studied the older woman for a moment. "You don't like Sonia, do you, Wyn? Yet you've worked so hard for her all these years."

"Correction, love. I've worked for *you.*" Wyn scooped up Rachael's shirt and jeans for the wash. "Matt and I were sunk as soon as we saw you. A motherless little five-year-old with huge blue eyes and lovely manners. A little princess, Matt said. We could see all your stepmother's love and attention was reserved for Scotty. We wanted to be around for *you.*"

"And aren't I glad?" Rachael breathed fervently. "You're my family, Wyn. I've always had you and Matt."

"So that's why we're worried now. Curt, too. I think he's come to put a stop to your workin' yourself to death. It's about time you took your rightful place as the beautiful daughter of this house!"

THEY ATE in the cedar-paneled formal dining room, the three of them at one end of a table that could accommodate twenty-two. It was all very grand and somewhat unnecessary. Paintings hung about the walls, valuable paintings—still lifes, landscapes. An enormous picture of galloping horses hung over the fireplace. Sonia had directed that only one of the chandeliers be turned on, but at least the actual dinner setting was awash with light from the candles. Pink roses in a silver bowl cast a splash of color, as did the rich, gold-embellished blue border on the Limoges china. It was a gracious scene, Rachael had to admit, but the informal dining room adjacent to the kitchen would have made less work for Wyn. The large, cheerful room with its gateleg table and set of eight Windsor chairs was nice enough for even their distinguished guest.

In the soft flattering light, Sonia didn't look a day over thirty. Blond, elegant, scented. Her pink crepe dress matched the lovely flush of the roses. Rachael realized that under different circumstances Sonia could have seemed a perfectly appropriate companion for Curt. Personable. Beautiful. Maybe a few years older, but by reason of his palpable air of authority, it wasn't a jarring age gap. The moment Rachael realized it, she all but shielded her eyes. A romance between Sonia and Curt Carradine was more than she could bear. It was a reaction that came from a lot of different reasons—she didn't want her father's memory betrayed, she genuinely didn't want Sonia to get hurt, and she didn't want Carradine interfering with Miriwin. And there were other reasons she couldn't look at too closely....

Tonight Sonia had decided on four courses. A light cheese-and-chives soufflé, succulent beef fillets with mushrooms and fresh vegetables from the kitchen gardens, a choice of Wyn's famous apple strudel or some black forest ice cream, and a cheese platter to finish off the Grange Hermitage Rachael's father had so enjoyed. Now Sonia sat in Alex Munro's place looking more like the mistress of Miriwin than she ever had before. In some ways, Rachael saw now, her father's attitude to Sonia had almost bordered on the paternalistic. Perhaps Sonia in a curious sense felt liberated. She did appear hell-bent on a new life.

Seated opposite Curt, Rachael was aware that his topaz glance was on her frequently. Not to admire Wyn's job on her hair or her best dress with the bold, splashy print but to check on how much she ate. He might have been watching a toddler in a highchair.

"How old am I, Curt?" She laid down her knife and fork.

"Twenty-three, as you recently reminded me." He smiled at her, a lethal smile that sent a shiver through her.

"So why are you watching every bite I take?"

"Forgive me, Rachael!" He spread his tanned, elegant hands. "I couldn't care less if you're just pushing it around on your plate. It doesn't bother me that you're starting to look decidedly frail or that you were too weak to even stand up by yourself this afternoon!"

"A touch of anorexia," Sonia suggested.

"Well, someone's got a touch of it," Rachael said smartly, "and it's not *me.*" Sonia had been on a very strict diet for years.

"Brighten my evening and have something," Curt said. "Perhaps Wyn's strudel."

"You're so...persuasive I just might." It was true her once healthy appetite had deserted her. She knew that at some time in the future it would come back, but for now she was grieving, and she appeared to be grieving alone.

Sonia resumed her dialogue with Curt, smiling brilliantly and emptying her wineglass rather too quickly. No doubt at all—Curt gave her quite a buzz, Rachael thought wryly, and he did look superb and perfectly at ease in her company. It was much too hot for him to wear a jacket, so he wore a beautiful, white, collarless designer shirt that threw his crow-black hair and darkly polished skin into high relief. It was criminal for a man to be so attractive! Sonia couldn't take her eyes off him, obviously delighted with his searing charm. Gone was the circumspection of a grieving widow. This was strictly man-woman stuff.

Where has all the pain gone? Rachael wondered dazedly. Hadn't Sonia ever been happy with her father? Alex Munro had given his wife plenty of freedom, plenty of money. She'd taken several annual trips to Sydney where she had family and a wide circle of society friends; there'd been frequent stints overseas, especially Hong Kong, where she always spent lavishly. Mostly for herself. She'd been very young when they'd married. Barely twenty to Alex Munro's thirty-four. She was young still, and sexually attractive. Not the sort of woman to remain a widow long. But she was too old for Curt, Rachael considered, and mad to think otherwise. Curt could have his pick of the most eligible young women in the country, some of them extraordinarily intelligent and beautiful.

"What are you thinking about so intensely, Rachael?" Curt's voice startled her.

"She hasn't heard a word we've been saying," Sonia added with a thread of sarcasm.

"I was thinking about the old days," Rachael said quietly. "How hard Dad worked. How much he loved this place. Life seems meaningless without him."

It plainly wasn't what Sonia wanted to hear. She drew a sharp breath and her features tightened. "We'll get through this, Rachael," she said firmly. "It does no good to dwell on things we can't change."

"On the other hand, feelings have to be worked out." Curt chose to intervene. "Grieving is necessary. There was a strong bond between you and your father, Rachael."

"Stronger still between Scott and his father," Sonia maintained, "yet Scott has learned to let go. Rachael was too emotionally attached to her father. She should have become independent long ago. Like Scott. He doesn't have this . . . this mania for the land."

"Then why did Dad leave him Miriwin?" Rachael asked passionately, her deeply blue eyes flashing.

"That's an absurd question, Rachael, and you know it." Sonia looked at her coldly. "Your father adored Scott, his only son. Curt will understand that. So naturally he inherited."

"You're not going to suggest Scotty's in Curt's league?" Rachael challenged. "If we're talking about mania for the land, you must see Curt shares it."

"Please, Rachael, say no more. You're upsetting me and disturbing our guest." She gazed at her stepdaughter repressively.

Rachael shrugged, her emotions still out of control. "Curt can take his chances like everyone else. You might also consider how your comments affect me."

"You've both been through a traumatic time." Curt gave the women a soothing look. "And, Rachael, you never have to worry about what you say to me. Don't bottle it up. You know, I think it would be very helpful if you could get away for a holiday. You desperately need one. It so happens the beach house is empty. We hire a married couple who act as caretakers. They do a great job, and they could look after your needs. A complete change would benefit you."

Instantly Sonia lit up. "What a lovely thought, Curt!"

"The problem is I don't want to go," Rachael said flatly. "There are too many things here to sort out."

"Really?" Sonia's voice rose.

"Look for yourself, Sonia. The paperwork has piled up. It has to be dealt with. And Matt can't spare me right now."

Sonia had lost her soft flush. "You seem to have forgotten Scott will be home soon."

Rachael shook her head. "I couldn't go anywhere right now." *Not with you two in collusion,* she thought.

Sonia leaned toward Curt. "You see what I mean now? I've urged Rachael to go away for a break. She's so much in need of it."

"Strange, I've never heard it suggested." Rachael was stung. They'd been discussing her, but she wasn't going to be manipulated. She didn't need a holiday. Not when there might be a plot already under way.

Sonia looked at her with an implacable expression. "That's a downright lie, Rachael. I've tried very hard to reason with you, but you're nothing if not stubborn. I assure you we'll get along fine without you."

"Which just goes to show what you don't know." Rachael said rudely, causing Sonia to cast her eyes down helplessly.

Curt intervened again. "I can see you're worried, Rachael, but let's see what we can do about it. I can supply some office help for the time you're away. It won't be so hard once Scott gets home. Sonia tells me he's been doing wonderfully with his studies, so by then he should have his degree in business management."

Wonderfully? Rachael carefully kept the surprise off her face. She knew Scott, and she doubted his studies were the focus of his concentration. But then, if Scott held up a bank, Sonia would say that it was wonderful, too.

Curt was talking to Sonia, the light glancing and gleaming on his face. "You're very welcome to join Rachael, Sonia, if she cares to go, only I have a party lined up I was counting on you to attend. A welcome for my cousin Philip and his new bride."

"That's marvelous!" Sonia's taut expression relaxed into delight. "I'm sure I'll enjoy it." Gracefully she covered his hand with her own.

Rachael felt a profound desire to hide under the table.

AFTER DINNER Rachael helped Wyn clear away the dishes then went for a walk. Let Sonia entertain their guest. It was clearly what *she* preferred; maybe it was his preference, too. No wonder Sonia wanted her to go away all of a sudden. Curt was always charming to women, but Sonia could be heading for disappointment if she expected a serious romance. And what were Curt's motives? If he wanted Miriwin, would he be shameless enough to use Sonia's obvious attraction to get it? He was used to steamrolling people, but Rachael had every intention of standing up for herself, protecting her own interests. Still, the idea of a few weeks at the beach was tantalizing. The bait dangled before her nose.

The hot winds of day had given way to a flower-scented stillness. The stars above her glittered in the black velvet sky. Rachael looked up, remembering all the *Dreamtime* stories. The Milky Way streamed across the center of the sky like a diamond river, the final resting place of the Elders. The windblown stars were their twinkling campfires. The Great Crocodile swam in the sparkling river, the big stars forming his spine and the curve of his tail. The Southern Cross hung above the sand hills, the star farthest south, a star of the first magnitude, pointing to the South Pole. The desert people believed the Southern Cross was the footprint of Waluwara, the great wedge-tailed eagle. Alpha and Beta centauri were his throwing sticks, the coal sack, his nest. As a child Rachael had spent a lot of time listening, as rapt as any aboriginal child. The earth was her spirit life, the sky her resting place. This was what Scotty and Sonia couldn't understand. Her dreaming place held her like a magnet.

When Rachael returned and stood in the open doorway of her father's favorite room, Curt and Sonia were still talking. About what? Rachael called good-night. Sonia gave a little start, as though she'd totally forgotten her step-daughter's existence, which she probably had. But Curt, ever the gentleman, came to his feet, golden eyes moving over her appraisingly.

"I think you qualify for a good night's sleep." It was a strangely intimate glance as though he was seeing her in a new light. Had she finally succeeded in jolting him into an awareness of her as an adult?

"Good night, Rachael," Sonia called, a command almost palpable in her voice. It was exactly the tone she'd used when the young Rachael had wanted to linger to talk to her father.

She had to take it then, but not now. "Did you speak to Matt about the helicopter?" she asked Curt directly.

"I did, Rachael, and he's endlessly grateful. It will make short work of what would be a very long and exhausting muster."

"You're very efficient, Curt. I wouldn't like to get in your way if you were planning a course of action."

"I doubt you could, Rachael," he said countering her thrust. "Have a sleep-in. We'll be starting very early in the morning."

AROUND MIDNIGHT she heard them coming upstairs, then a few minutes later the lights went on in their best guest room. They flooded out across the veranda, turning the white lace curtains of Rachael's bedroom a luminescent gold. Before Rachael totally gave in to exhaustion there were things she needed to know. She got up, immediately shouldering into a pink embroidered robe Scott had bought for her. Things were moving too quickly for her liking. It was a good time to speak to Curt. Perhaps the only time.

Rachael padded silently through the French doors, glancing along the length of the veranda. The moon had come out, bathing the gardens in a milk-opal radiance. She could see the silver ribbon of creek that encircled the main compound. It was narrow, but in flood could run great volumes of water, rising around the compound like a moat. A long frond of golden cane thrashed her in the face, and she put up her hand uncertainly. The impetus that had gotten her out of bed wasn't nearly so strong now. He might already be preparing for sleep. A vision of that lean splendid body naked abruptly assailed her, and she shook her head in disbelief. Images of naked men normally didn't affect her, but that one certainly did. It was as if a new part of her had been revealed.

Still padding quietly, Rachael felt her heart give a mad buck as Curt walked out onto the veranda. Perhaps he wanted to enjoy the effect of the white moonlight on the sleeping garden and the infinite distances beyond. He moved to the balcony and placed his hands on the balustrade; then he spoke aloud, startling her. "If we're going to talk, Rachael, we'd better do it now." He turned in her direction and she moved forward into the light.

"Can your ears hear a pin drop?" she asked.

"What do you think?"

"I suppose the answer's yes. In another life you must have been a lion."

"So, do you want to take your chances walking into my den?"

"I thought we'd stay out on the veranda." Wariness was in every line of her body.

"I'm inclined to agree. You look delicious in that silk robe."

"As a matter of fact, it's satin. Scotty bought it for me. Picked it out himself."

"He has excellent taste. Shall we relax in a chair, Rachael? You seem to be out of breath."

"Amusing!" She took a seat in a wicker chair, resting her hands on the arms. "You can't see me as anything but a silly schoolgirl, can you?"

"Silly?" He laughed. "Who would ever refer to you in that way? You were really very sweet."

"Sweet, silly even, but not *stupid*," Rachael said tartly.

"All right, get it off your chest." He took the chair opposite her. "I knew at dinner you wanted to fire some questions at me."

"I'll endure your patronizing me, Curt, if you'll tell me one thing."

"Anything, Rachael." His golden eyes glowed in the half-light. "No sense sitting around brooding."

"You're so right!" A flash of hostility showed on her expressive face. "You would tell me if you were thinking of offering for Miriwin? It's weighing heavily on my mind."

For a moment he looked angry, arrogant, ruthless. All the things his grandfather had been purported to be. "So that's what this is all about?"

"Well, it's not a seduction scene," she snapped. "Miriwin may be just another deal to you, but it's my home!"

"Your father left it to Scott." Curt answered so bluntly Rachael drew back, stunned.

"I never knew you were cruel."

"There's a lot you don't know about me," he told her tersely. "I can be tough when I have to. But, Rachael, I'd never be deliberately cruel to you. It's hard, I know, to face the realities of life. Whether one questions your father's judgment or not, he did leave the fate of Miriwin in Scott's hands. You could have contested the will.''

Rachael pressed her fingers to her eyes. ''Sonia would hate me forever, though I guess I could live with that. I did think about contesting it, but in the end I decided I wouldn't go against Dad's wishes. I always was an extraordinarily dutiful daughter. It didn't help me much.''

''So you're stuck with your twenty percent,'' Curt said. ''Decisions have to be made all through life. Some big, some small. You've made yours.''

''I want Scotty to come home.''

''You're assuming he's going to take up his inheritance?''

''I'm *counting* on it,'' Rachael said.

''He hasn't shown the least interest in Miriwin to date.''

''He's young!'' Rachael spoke with intense loyalty.

Curt's brilliant gaze was skeptical. ''Love of the land is in the blood. It shows up very early. Scott's always going to want an easy life. He won't get it on a cattle station.''

''Have you said this to Sonia?'' she challenged.

''Do you think she'd listen?''

''Come on. She'd listen to you.''

''Why?'' he asked shortly, responding to her taunting tone.

Rachael shrugged a slim shoulder. ''She admires you. Respects you.''

''Sonia regards her son as perfect. You know that, Rachael. I would have thought it was a sore subject. She's never been particularly indulgent with you.''

''You mean you've noticed?'' She couldn't suppress the sarcasm.

''Once or twice,'' he said starkly. ''I'd like you to go away for that holiday, Rachael. You and Sonia need a break from one another.''

Rachael flushed. "Another thing you've noticed?"

"It's hard not to. Even I have begun to notice you're a woman now. An adult. You have your own opinions, know your own mind. It's bound to make for difficulties."

"So you want to shunt me off?"

"Don't be ridiculous! I care about you and your welfare."

"And while I'm away, you and Sonia can talk over Miriwin's future?"

"Thank you, Rachael, for your high regard."

"So you deny you have any interest in Miriwin at all?"

"Hell, would you like me to take a lie-detector test?"

"No, just level with me."

He shifted slightly so he was staring right at her. "Running the Carradine Pastoral Company is my whole life. I'm committed not only to holding on to what was left to me but building on it. Expanding the empire, if you like. Miriwin in its heyday was a fine station, but your father suffered a lot of reversals and didn't always make the right decisions. If Miriwin was ever put on the market—willingly, by all of you—I'd acquire it. That's the way it works. You're smart enough to see all the advantages from my point of view. The issue simply hasn't been raised. It never will be by *me*. I'm resigned to the fact that Miriwin means everything to you. As for my discussions with Sonia, they aren't your business. Try to understand this. Sonia feels weighed down by all the responsibilities of station life. She wasn't reared to it as you were, and she's never learned to live it through all the years of her marriage. She's missing your father and she doesn't know how to cope."

"I thought she was coping perfectly well tonight." Rachael gave a brittle laugh.

"And what is that supposed to mean? No, look at me." His hand shot out, capturing her chin.

"You know damned well," she said succinctly.

He released her in apparent disgust. "Clearly you're still seeing things in the wrong light. I thought you had more sense."

"What's sense got to do with it?" Rachael asked with spirit. "You're here so frequently. Does Sonia invite you?"

"Naturally. Are you suggesting I'm making a nuisance of myself?" His tone was cutting.

"Frankly, I think you're manipulating us all." Rachael whirled to her feet. "You're not a kind man like your father. You're more like your wicked old grandfather!"

"Wicked old grandfather be damned!" Curt, too, stood up, towering over her. "Jock Munro was no saint, either."

"You mean he wasn't willing to be pushed off his land?" The breeze ruffled Rachael's hair so it blew in masses of curls around her fiery face. "You Carradines have been manipulating people for years. You're cattle kings. Empire builders. *You* have hundreds of people jumping at your every word. You're virtually a law unto yourself. Hell, you have more power than the prime minister and you have it for *life*. Another thing—you've never been known to pass up a good deal if there's one going. Sonia looks to you for support and advice. It would be so easy to drop a few hints."

His expression hardened. "Except that going behind your back doesn't sit well with me. You're an insulting little devil, aren't you?"

"I'm sorry, but this business is a weight pressing on my heart."

"There is no business, Rachael. Not if I can help it. I know you're having a difficult time and I'm trying to make allowances, but—"

"Difficult?" Rachael was so tired and upset she was dizzy. Tears clung to her thick, sooty lashes. "It's unutterable grief! Does no one else mourn Dad?"

He looked appalled. "Do they have to mourn in your way? Sometimes it's all people can do just to keep going. Your emotions run deep, but there's not a damned thing you can do about anyone whose feelings aren't so profound. I know you feel deeply wounded, but there's nothing to be gained in becoming so critical of Sonia. She's different from you."

Her face burned under his austere gaze. "You're saying now it's *my* fault? You're right, of course. You must do whatever you please. Who am I to stop you!"

"Yes, indeed!"

Something galvanic in his tone cut her breath short. She stood immobilized while he took hold of her, as though surrendering to some primitive impulse, long denied.

"What you need is a man's arms around you."

His golden eyes were riveted on hers, brilliant with a kind of harsh relish. She'd been imagining this very scenario since the age of sixteen, but the reality shocked her almost senseless. As her body came into contact with his, a woman's delicate curves against a man's hard strength, she was engulfed in heat, a great wave of desire that had her twisting and gasping, her breath coming ragged.

"Stop it this minute, Curt. I can't bear it!"

"No, Rachael!" he retorted, a crackle in his voice.

Athletic though she was, he controlled her struggles with no more than the lightest pressure, so that all of a sudden she stopped in amazement.

"What, given up already?" she heard him say tauntingly. "You're a maddening creature, Rachael. A lot more complex than I thought. An entrancing adolescent into a luminous little firebrand. A real hazard. Some men might find it exciting."

His spread fingers lifted her chin. She was speechless, half panting, then his mouth descended on hers, so masterfully, so magically, so broodingly warm and intimate, a shock wave tore up her spine and her mouth flowered in frantic response. She hardly knew what she was doing, taken so utterly by surprise. His hand slipped into the radiant mass of her hair. His other arm cradled her body and her head slipped into the crook of his shoulder as if it belonged there. The force of his energy encompassed her like a cloud, causing her trembling flesh to blush with color, then melt like wax.

She knew it then for what it was. The Carradine brand.

Her veins were glittering threads of fire. He moved them back into the shadows, his mouth still fused to hers. The kiss that had started out so long and hard deepened into such voluptuousness her body slumped against his. Surrendering to passion was an alarming thing. Dimly she became aware that someone was moaning softly. The sounds stopped as she drew breath.

In the space of a heartbeat he released her, his falling hand brushing her breast, inciting more ripples of sensation. Beneath her satin robe her nipples were tightly budded in arousal. She felt vulnerable beyond relief.

"So that's settled, I think," he said in a perfectly cool voice.

"What is?" she asked jaggedly, staring up into his face. "I don't think anything's settled. The fact is, you do as you please."

"Starting tonight," he said. "Kissing you was pure instinct. Up to now I've wrestled it down. It didn't seem right. Sweet little Rachael Munro. You may have done a terrible thing by reminding me you're twenty-three."

"It's more likely all part of your grand plan. Don't play me for a fool, Curt. Scott and Sonia might fall on your every word. I can't be so easily maneuvered."

"But of course you can," he said, in a compelling, ferociously sexy voice.

"I guess I deserved that," Rachael sighed.

"I'd say so," he agreed. "You could have stopped me any time you chose."

"Maybe I wanted to see what all the fuss was about."

"Fuss?" His strange eyes glittered. "I don't understand."

"You mean you haven't overheard yourself discussed? Curt Carradine, the most eligible bachelor in the country?"

He shrugged carelessly. "Should that make me feel guilty?"

"It might explain your high-handedness."

His gaze moved over her slowly. "I don't think you understand your own sexuality. It's as powerful as the scent of roses. But don't worry, I'm no predator feasting on little girls like you. After all, I remember you when you were in your high chair."

"And I remember you striding all around the place with your father. You had this tremendous air of being lord of all you surveyed. I used to think it was one of your attractions. Now I'm not so sure."

"You mean you think it's the past revisited? The Carradines and the Munros?"

Rachael nodded. "I'm afraid so. You're forceful and ambitious. In the right hands, Miriwin could be what it was before. It needs a big injection of capital, but you've got plenty of that. You won't need to take us over by force. You'll charm us, instead."

"Well, well!" He reached out and turned her toward the light. "You've given this a lot of thought."

"To be honest, it's only just occurred to me."

"Sure someone didn't put it into your head?" he asked shrewdly. "Matt must have heard a few of the rumors by now."

"It pays to check them out."

His hand brushed her cheek. "I told you before—I'm *not* going to be the one to take your home from you, Rachael. I know what that means."

"It means the same as if someone was trying to take Carrara from you."

"Except that I have full control of Carrara, and I'm the chairman of the Carradine Pastoral Company."

"All true." She dipped her head.

"Your father's will hurt you badly," he said somberly.

"What if it did!" She looked up. "All I really want is for the Munros to hold on to what's ours. What we fought and died for. You've got your cemetery on the hill, just as we have. Miriwin's our history. We've fought off the Carradines before."

"Don't you think you're getting a bit paranoid about it?"

"I can't believe you'd turn us out, Curt." Her heart was in her eyes.

"I would have thought I'd earned your trust."

She glanced away across the garden. "I've always trusted you in the past, but I'm having a bad time of it lately."

"You need a holiday," he said, his voice deep and persuasive. "It will give Sonia time to herself, as well."

Rachael could feel the anger rising in her. "Of course! That's the real issue. Pleasing Sonia."

"Oh, don't be so damned silly. I'm thinking of *you,* but I can't turn my back on Sonia, either."

"You don't have to come over *every* time she asks," Rachael flared. "Sonia's coming to depend on you. Unless you want the job, that's dangerous."

"Cool down," he said tersely. "I know what I'm doing. I'm speaking in the name of friendship, and I'm thinking of you both. Right now you need a complete break, and I suggest you take it. Look at me, Rachael."

"I'd rather not. I think more clearly when I'm not looking into your eyes."

"Well, I'm not going to talk to the back of your head."

"It's okay. I can hear you."

In answer he swung her around, grasping a thick coil of her hair. Physically it started happening again. The dizziness, the sweetness, the almost excruciating onslaught of sensation. When he touched her she was doomed. But that was her secret.

"Promise me you'll do as I say."

Shivers crept up the back of her neck. She was powerfully aware of the fascination of his voice. "I'm fine, really, here at home."

"No, you're not. Wyn and Matt agree with me."

"You're not a good influence around here." She tried to break away, but he tightened his grip, drawing her closer. "Let's strike a deal," she managed huskily. "I'll take myself off to your beach house if you curtail your meetings with Sonia. Believe it or not, she'll survive without you."

"With no trouble at all, I would expect," he said suavely.

"I'm too worried to be subtle. Is it a deal?"

"It is," he said. "But I think it might be more binding if we sealed it with a kiss."

"No, thanks."

"I insist on it, anyway." It was said matter-of-factly, yet he kissed her until her flesh dissolved.

CHAPTER THREE

RACHAEL SPENT the morning trying to focus her mind on the station accounts. It wasn't easy, given the events of the night before, but she struggled on. Bills had piled up alarmingly. She sorted them into various bundles, the topmost for immediate attention. There were personal bills for Sonia, as well—reminders of her stay with the Radfords at their Sydney harbor-side mansion. Sonia had managed to spend thousands of dollars on outfits and shoes when her huge, walk-in wardrobe was already dense with clothes. Why didn't she give some of them away? *She's never passed anything on to me,* Rachael thought with some amazement. I'm three inches taller, but we take the same size. Ah, well! Some of the discards were gorgeous, too.

She worked steadily until lunchtime, then went in search of a cup of coffee and a sandwich. She'd made up her mind to ride out to the ridge overlooking Devil's Gorge afterward. It was always exciting to see a good helicopter pilot in action. Bob Grafton, chief pilot for Grafton Helicopters, worked for Carrara, flagship of the Carradine empire, so she guessed it would be Bob on call today.

Sonia met her in the hallway, greeting her amiably. "Oh, there you are, Rachael. Is your nose out of joint at having to stay home? It's high time someone stepped in to stop you. I never thought it a good idea, your going on long musters with the men."

"They're all my friends," Rachael said. "I'm safer with them than I would be anywhere."

"Excuse me if I don't see it like that." Sonia laughed. "Men are lustful creatures. You do have a sexy way about you, though I must admit you don't trade on it. Come and join me for lunch. The house is terribly empty these days."

"I only want a sandwich."

"Then have a sandwich. Put a whole lot on it. Curt's right. You're starting to look lanky."

"Lanky? Did he really say that?"

"Something like it."

They walked together into the family dining room where lunch had been set up. Cold meats and a bowl of fresh garden salad. Sonia, in dazzling white today, seated herself near the picture window looking out over the rear gardens with their magnificent gum trees.

"It must be difficult forsaking all the excitement of the helicopter muster." She spoke in a light, satirical tone.

"Their loss." Rachael put a little ham and salad on her plate. "I thought I'd ride out and see them come in."

Immediately, waves of disapproval hit the atmosphere, chilling it by several degrees. "I'd advise you to stay put," Sonia said. "Curt has left instructions."

"*Curt* has! Tyrannical old him!" Rachael groused. "He can't tell me what to do."

"Don't start that all over again." Sonia broke a small piece off a freshly baked roll. "I don't know where we'd be without Curt."

"Maybe better off. We'd have to go ahead under our own steam."

"Thank you, Rachael, but I've led much too idle a life. It was awfully good of him to offer you his beach house. I do hope you're going to accept."

"I can't go anywhere right now. There's too much to do. *Really*, Sonia."

"No one is indispensable," Sonia said sharply. "Your father never thought he could spare a minute out of his life, either. Sometimes I think living at Miriwin is like being in hell!"

"It's the drought, Sonia." Rachael put out a hand to her stepmother, who didn't respond.

"I don't think I can handle much more of it," Sonia confessed. "This heat and no rain. And all the time we're getting deeper and deeper into debt."

"You could have remembered that when you raided the Sydney boutiques. But if we all tighten our belts, things will work out, eventually. Even Carrara is hurting."

"We can't judge Miriwin by Carrara's standards," Sonia said, ignoring the reference to her extravagance. "What are we holding on for, anyway? That's what I'd like to know. What's going to change around here?"

"The rain will change everything, Sonia. Make things good again. The future is looking bright for the beef industry. Curt is a tireless worker as head of the Cattlemen's Union. If we all pull together, we'll get through the bad times."

"God, how you sound like your father!" Sonia wailed. "You'd think Miriwin was the center of the world. Now that your father's gone, I can't stand it. The loneliness and the money-juggling. People interfering in our affairs. Those damned accountants wanting more and more information. Next it will be the tax office. This isn't what I want, Rachael. I've never had to concern myself with how the station actually worked."

"You could learn, Sonia. You're a smart woman. It isn't all that difficult."

"Except I have no interest in it whatsoever. I'm a woman, Rachael. Not a woman masquerading as a man."

"I suppose that's a shot at me," Rachael said, hiding her hurt. "I haven't had much choice. Why isn't Scotty home?"

"Surely you recognize he has commitments."

"Parties?"

Sonia remained loyal. "Scott has made lots and lots of useful friends. One needs them in life. You surely don't think he's going to bury himself here?"

"I thought that was the whole idea!" Rachael said bluntly. "Scotty is the principal heir. You weren't subtle about pushing his claim."

"So what?" Sonia shrugged. "My only option, as I've told you before. Good heavens, you'd think your twenty percent was a pittance. It will keep you comfortably. You're not homeless, penniless. Would you mind pressing the buzzer? I'd like some coffee."

Clearly Sonia had no more to say.

CURLING CLOUDS OF DUST rose from the south and the southwest, coiling themselves into lazy lariats in the cobalt blue sky. The mob was coming in from Devil's Gorge, and Rachael urged the mare to the crest of the fiery red ridge that overlooked the bowl-shaped valley. In the Wet this particular valley was a giant carpet of pink and blue wildflowers. Now it was a quivering ocean of tinder-dry yellow grass that greened to an emerald line along the banks of the main channel of the river, the station's lifeblood.

The mirage was playing tricks with her eyes. Arrows of light were leaping and dancing across the valley floor in a wild corroboree. Even in the far distance, the dense line of tall trees, black in the hot glare, had lost contact with the ground. They floated in the weird silver light. As she quietly sat her horse, distant sounds reached her. The lowing of cattle. It was just an hour since she'd sighted the helicopter, like a yellow toy banking westward toward Carrara Downs.

Loose stones rattled down from the crest as the first of the black dots came into sight. Gradually the quivering dots became cattle. Rachael estimated around six or seven hundred head. She could see the shadowy figures of riders flanking them, several bringing up the rear. Although the worst of the day's heat was over, the mob was moving slowly in the interests of smooth progress to the holding yards at Totem Creek. They should reach there by dusk.

After the disturbing events of last night, she couldn't get Curt out of her mind. His hold was so profound it shattered her calm. She had to face the fact, too, that Sonia was giving in to a long-hidden infatuation with Curt Carradine. An infatuation that could influence Miriwin's fate, and Rachael knew she was powerless to do anything about it. Whatever *her* feelings, Sonia was going to live her own life.

If only Scott would come home! Rachael desperately needed to talk to him. She had to impress on him the need to carry on the Munro name and tradition. It had always seemed so important to her, yet Scotty had privately confessed that he often found Miriwin "dreadfully boring." For that matter, it was a favorite expression of Sonia's. Could it be true that all they'd wanted was the money? To Rachael it was an abuse of trust.

As the phalanx of cattle moved across the valley she rode down the ridge to meet them. Distances in the mirage were deceptive. The herd was a lot closer than she'd first thought. She started to increase the mare's pace, keeping well to the right of the cattle as they continued their northerly trek. They were well under control, not strung out across the valley floor. They would have hated coming over the stony terrain on the way back from the gorge, but as a mob that included a good many cleanskins they were behaving like a well-drilled army. In the good times it would have been hard to shift them from the lush valley grazing, but the yellow stubble wasn't holding a lot of interest.

She could make out the riders clearly. Nat Roberts, the new jackaroo, was up front because of his lack of experience and riding skills. Matt and the other men brought up the flank and rear in case some of the cattle decided to bolt. Even at a distance it was possible to identify Curt. He was a superb horseman. He never slouched, and his lean, superbly toned body had an individuality no one could fail to recognize.

She rode on. Soon the mob would smell the water and become restless, especially in the heat. It was the stockman's job to keep them walking until they reached Totem Creek. That was the plan. Apart from the fact that cattle couldn't travel in the heat if they drank too much, the main channel of the Muru ran fairly deep at all times.

Nat was weaving back and forth in front of the mob like a weekend cowboy. Rachael, although she liked him, didn't think he would ever make a good stockman, let alone a bushman. A few weeks back he had gotten lost two miles from camp, and Paddy, their head ringer, had dubbed him "Scatty Nat." She could see Curt move up on him, probably to tell him to cut out the antics. The whole idea was to keep the mob tight and on the planned trail. At this point Curt saw Rachael and lifted an arm in salute.

Why, oh, why had he given her that spellbinding kiss? Wasn't life complicated enough?

A chastised Nat caught sight of her, too, and without warning stood up in the saddle and let out an earsplitting *cooee,* the bushman's greeting. It vibrated across the valley like the high-pitched whine of a Learjet and then some. Rachael and the experienced stockmen were struck dumb, but the mob took it as the signal to stampede. From a slow plod they slammed into full speed, their frightening bellowing setting up such a commotion the great flocks of corellas adorning the trees exploded into the air, screeching their wrath.

Rachael felt a moment of sheer terror, then kicked her mare into a gallop. A good workhorse but never fast, the mare was so terrified she took off like a shot. Rachael risked turning her head briefly only to see a phalanx of cattle hell-bent on the water and mindless of anything in its path. The river was the only place to go, but having the mob come in after her presented huge problems. God, was Nat dumb!

The front-runners went flying past her with a thundering of hooves. Out of the corner of her eye she could see Matt almost parallel with her but too far to the right. The mob had spread out dramatically, changing direction and heading instinctively for the water. Rachael's heart shook with fright as she pushed her horse to the limit. The mare was tiring badly, and she had a mental flash of herself lying trampled on the ground.

A rider materialized out of nowhere, slamming alongside the agonized mare and lifting Rachael clear of the saddle with a galvanic effort and a thunderous *"Jump!"* For an instant she was airborne, then she was firmly in the saddle in front of Curt. His arm held her like a vice, and she wondered if her ribs would crack. They were galloping head-long toward the channel's edge. They were going in. What other choice was there? Rachael braced herself for the plunge. In the distance a gun went off but she wasn't witness to the main mob shuddering to a stop, as usual acting like one. The ground had run out. She was sailing into the murky green depths of the channel, Curt incredibly keeping his hold on her. Rachael thought dazedly he had to be Superman.

They both came up spewing water like whales. The front-running cattle were milling and lowing around them, aware they were in disgrace. Nat, to avoid the barrage of abuse aimed at him, was running along the bank chasing Curt's bay gelding and Rachael's mare as they swam downstream.

"God Almighty!" Curt shouted in utter frustration. His golden eyes blazed and he looked truly fierce. "Are you all right, Rachael?"

"I'm not sure. I'll tell you when I get my hat." No way was she going to lose it. It was her best.

"Rachael?" he thundered after her but she didn't look back. The akubra was gently sailing downstream with something that looked like a massive frog parked on the crown.

Clearly disgusted, Curt struck out after her, not even looking at her as he cut past like a shark. He retrieved the hat and threw off its passenger, which skipped along the surface of the water.

"Put it on if it's so valuable," he rasped when he was alongside.

"Don't tell me what to do." Ridiculously Rachael planted the wet akubra on her head, then swam for the bank.

He reached it first, of course, deliberately spurting past her. Sometimes she couldn't tolerate a man's physical superiority. No wonder they were so damned macho.

"Here, Rachael, give me your hand." He leaned down to her, heaving her out of the water with lavish strength. They were staring at each other hard. Almost like combatants. Rachael tugged her wet shirt away from her body, excruciatingly aware she wasn't wearing a bra, and her shirt was nearly transparent when wet. Why had she gone to the bother of looking more presentable when all that was waiting for her was a dunking?

"You've lost your hat, too," she told him.

"I don't rate my hats as highly as you do. Didn't I tell you to stay home?"

"Oh, spare me the big-boss act," she said, highly offended. "I didn't have anything to do with this. It was that darn fool Nat trying to win a *cooee* contest."

Curt's handsome face was set in hard, emphatic lines. "He practically got you killed."

"So there's no need to come down on *me* like a ton of bricks!" Rachael's blue eyes flashed. "Please don't take it out on Nat, either. I'm sure he learned a lesson. He didn't mean anything."

"That would have been a great comfort if you'd been trampled."

Rachael threw up her hands. "I was in the wrong place at the wrong time. It's over. I suggest we forget it."

"I will," Curt said harshly, "when my heart stops thumping. You'll have to get yourself a better horse. The mare was no help at all."

"She's cool in a crisis, which is more than I can say for you. Why are you so angry? It isn't the worst thing that's ever happened!"

"To picture you dead or disabled? Come off it, Rachael. You scared the living daylights out of me. I bet Matt's having a heart attack right now."

Rachael briefly closed her eyes. "Listen, I'm sorry. Give me a break, all right?"

"God, Rachael," he said quietly.

Her heart gave a funny bump, but she rushed on regardless. "To give the devil his due, you saved my life. What for? To chuck me off my own land?"

There was no mistaking his anger. His eyes narrowed to mere slits and his lean body tensed. "Don't start *that* again. I'm in no mood for it. We're both soaking wet. Let's go back to the house."

"That's not a bad idea for you. *I* mightn't want to."

His look made her legs tremble. "You've got a big problem, Rachael," he drawled softly. "You'd better try to straighten it out. Fast."

"I think I'm fine."

Matt interrupted their odd little confrontation, limping toward them, leading the two horses he'd retrieved. "That bloody fool boy!" he swore. "I ought to give him the sack, only I can't guarantee he won't land somebody else in a worse mess. You all right, Rachael, honey? I swear I'll have nightmares about this."

"No worries, Matt!" Rachael said cheerfully.

"Thanks to Curt." Matt nodded emphatically several times. "Don't let your ego suffer, girl." He turned confidingly to Curt. "Rachael has a lot of pride."

"Tell me about it." Curt shrugged. "Thanks for rescuing the horses. If you're okay here, Matt, I'll take Rachael on home."

"Hey, don't let me keep ya!" Matt looked at them as though noting their drenched appearance for the first time. "We'll get the mob settled, then we'll mozzie on. Walk 'em slow. Thanks a million, Curt, for your help. It's greatly appreciated. Thank you, too, for savin' Rachael here. I love that girl. I can't think what I'd do if anything happened to her. Don't worry about that fool boy, either. I'll straighten him out."

"Enter him in the next *cooee* contest," Rachael suggested, not altogether in fun.

Matt nodded, apparently taking her seriously. "That sounds fine. He's not gonna make a stockman."

THE HOT WIND tugged at her hair and Rachael let it fly, a brilliant pennant over her shoulder.

"You'll have to put your hat on soon," Curt warned her. He was concerned, she knew, about the full impact of the sun.

"I will. It's nearly dry." Rachael raised a hand to the glowing masses, tightened by the river water into deep waves and springing curls. Her yellow shirt was nearly dry and her moleskins were comfortably warm on her legs. By the time they reached the homestead, her clothes would be thoroughly dried out. The flats stretched before them, a yellow canvas broken by stands of bauhinias that flowered even in the most severe drought. The mare, nervous after her ordeal, was acting up now and then, so Rachael had to soothe her with pats and soft words.

"Do you think it will ever rain?" she asked Curt as she crammed her akubra back on her head.

"It'll have to." He looked grim. "We're reaching desperation point. In my grandfather's day, the aboriginals used to sing the rain in. Extraordinarily it worked. We've lost a lot with the passing of the old culture. These people have been here sixty thousand years. There's nothing they don't know about the land and how to preserve it. Remember Kidgee, one of the elders? He's sure we're going to get a heavy rain soon. When I ask him what's his reasoning he tells me his guardian spirit says so."

"That's good enough for me." Rachael's reply was instantaneous. "I've seen too much to brush off what the guardian spirits have to say."

"The heat doesn't seem to bother you," he observed, his glance moving over her clean-cut profile.

"Sonia *hates* it. She's finding it particularly distressing at the moment."

"Yet she looks as cool as ever."

"I wonder why she ever married Dad?" Rachael found herself musing aloud, to her shock.

"You don't think she loved him?"

"I never said that." Rachael shook her head. "They seemed reasonably happy together. Dad certainly gave her everything she wanted. Whenever she got bored or restless he let her go off on her travels. She was always much more cheerful when she got home. Not that she's ever felt at home here. It must be strange to settle in a place where you're constantly at war with the environment. She hasn't even *tried* to enjoy it here for the past ten years. I remember when she used to go riding, for instance. She doesn't anymore. I have a feeling once Scotty takes over, Sonia might go back to Sydney. At least for the summer."

"You could be right," Curt agreed. "She has family and friends there. She's still young."

Rachael searched his face hesitantly. "You think she'll remarry?"

His expression didn't change. "I get that impression."

"I hope she doesn't rush into anything. Sonia is very vulnerable right now."

"I'm aware of that, Rachael." He directed a brilliant glance at her.

"I made an attempt to tell her that, but it wasn't well received."

He nodded matter-of-factly. "Very few people like to be told, something so personal. And your relationship with Sonia was never easy."

Rachael drew a short, shallow breath. "You could say that. Sonia idolizes Scotty, but strangely enough she's not a maternal woman. At least her maternal instincts didn't extend to me."

"She might have managed better had your father not been so wretched over the loss of your mother. He never got over it. In some ways, I think, it colored his existence."

Rachael swung her head toward him, dumbfounded. "How can you say that, Curt? He never said a word."

"Very, very occasionally, he did. It could only have increased Sonia's ambivalent feelings toward you."

"Tell me." She was oddly upset yet deeply curious.

"I recall a conversation just before Christmas. He said in Sonia's hearing that he would never forget your mother's *radiance*. It just came out of the blue, but was deeply revealing, don't you think? I imagine Sonia found it quite painful. From the expression on her face, it wasn't the first time something like that had slipped out. I've heard your father speak of your mother with tears in his eyes. For your father to *weep!*" His tone was wondering.

"If he did, I never saw it," Rachael said. "I don't remember any of this. I had no idea."

"How could you evaluate the situation as a child? In the main your father never did talk about that tragic phase of his life and obviously never in front of you. But it was always with him. You're said to be the image of your mother. Even I remember her rose-colored hair and violet eyes. It was a face full of intelligence and fire. Difficult to forget."

"One would have thought it would make Dad more indulgent with me, but he was always stern. Maybe he directed some of his inner rage at me. I lived while my mother died. It's not so hard to believe. At least it explains a few things."

"I liked your father, Rachael," Curt said, "but he had some dark place in his soul. I know he loved you, even if he wasn't able to express it as well as he should." They rode in silence for a few minutes, then he spoke again. "It recently occurred to me there used to be a portrait of your mother at the top of the stairs, Rachael. Whatever happened to it?"

"Lord, Curt, how would I know?" She was startled by this new piece of information. "When did you last see it?"

"I saw it whenever my father and I came to call. It must have come down around the time your father married Sonia. Understandable, I suppose. But someone must know where it is. If so, it's yours. I've been looking for a quiet moment to tell you, but there never seems to be one."

"How extraordinary!" Rachael stared out at the silver, dancing mirage. "Perhaps it went to my grandparents. Dad never took me to visit them, you know. When I was old enough to go by myself, it was too late. Grandfather had had a stroke and no one thought he recognized me. I did, though. I swear there was some pressure on my hand. It must have been an enormous blow for my grandparents to lose their only child, then be deprived of their granddaughter. I hate to say it, but Dad behaved very badly toward them. My grandmother died before I could make it up to her. It's terrible to discover things like that about the past. I wanted to see Dad as perfect."

"You don't now?"

"In some ways he betrayed me," Rachael said simply. "Scotty always got to go home to Sydney with Sonia. What was the problem with my grandparents?"

Curt glanced across at her somberly. "It was said at the time that your grandparents blamed your father for your mother's death. Your father apparently insisted his first child be born on Miriwin. Had she been hospitalized, most likely she would have been saved. It's too tragic to think about. Your father kept very much to himself after your mother died. He had women in looking after you until he met Sonia two years later. People were stunned when he came back from Sydney with a young bride. A lot of people thought Sonia a highly unsatisfactory stepmother for you. And then it was only a matter of months before she was pregnant with Scott. It couldn't have been easy for her, either."

"No. Yet she was determined to become Mrs. Alexander Munro of Miriwin Station. She told me herself."

"Does anyone really know at nineteen what he or she wants to be?"

"You like Sonia, don't you?" Rachael asked, head-on.

"Surely I wouldn't come here if I didn't."

Was there a flicker of a taunt in his voice?

Rachael looked up at a frieze of black swans flying low against the opal sky. "I do wish Scotty would come home."

"Is that going to solve your problems?"

"At least we could talk things out."

"That's true." Curt adjusted his akubra against the blinding sun. "Meanwhile you could take your holiday. The world won't come to a halt if you take some time off. I can send someone over to help out in the office.

Rachael threw him a speaking look. "No, thank you. You know enough of our secrets." She paused. "I'd really like to go, Curt. The thought of plunging into the surf is wonderful in all this heat, but I want to be here when Scotty gets home."

"You'll see Scott when the festivities die down," Curt said dryly. "They'd be at their height at the moment."

"I have to think it over."

He gave her a brief nod. "All right. Tell me before I leave this afternoon."

CHAPTER FOUR

DESPITE A FEW QUALMS, Rachael enjoyed every minute of her stay at Curt's beach house on the Queensland coast some hundred miles from Brisbane. It was a stunning building poised atop a headland looking out over the glorious blue ocean windward, with the river and hinterland on the leeward side. Inside was all space and freedom. Ingenious doors that slid out of sight threw open the entire living area to the expansive deck with its incomparable views and luscious sea breezes. Palm trees and golden canes towered all around her. The garden also boasted a magnificent poinciana in full, brilliant color, as well as hundreds of ferns livened by dense areas of white and yellow daisies, a color scheme currently in vogue with Leo, who looked after the garden, while Marie, his wife, looked after the house. As caretakers they were treasures. They attended to Rachael's every need with unobtrusive efficiency and kindness.

Each day dawned more beautiful than the last. In the morning she swam in the crystal-clear surf. In the afternoon, since she'd been given the use of a small car, she explored the delightful resort village and the rich, volcanic hinterland with its teeming orchards of citrus and tropical fruits. There were the mountain villages to interest her with their arts and crafts. And famous little restaurants where one came for lunch and stayed on for dinner. From a high vantage point in the National Park she looked out at the fantastic shapes of the Glass House Mountains, named in

1770 by Captain James Cook after the glass-blowing furnaces of Whitby. One great tor after another rose in isolated splendor from the thick jungle floor, their aboriginal names faintly scary, as were their distorted cone shapes. It was a spellbinding sight.

Rachael was feeling so much better away from Miriwin's tensions. She'd begun to relax in the healing power of her beautiful environment. At night she sometimes watched television or read through the pile of glossy magazines and best-sellers bought especially for her. Once or twice she had tried strolling around the village, a hive of activity at night, but found herself the target of a little too much male attention. Besides, having time to read was a wonderful luxury. But usually she was so pleasantly tired after the day's activities, she fell into a deep peaceful sleep that lasted until around seven the next morning, when the surf called her.

It was marvelous to run down the stairs that led to the beach, to race across the white sand, to dive straight under the first breaker. Her appetite, too, had been stimulated by the sea and salt, and she'd put on a few necessary pounds. There had been talk of Scott's driving up from Brisbane to join her one weekend, but at the last moment, when she was so looking forward to it and preparations had been made, he rang to say something had come up. It wasn't the first time Scott had disappointed her, but it didn't change her love for him. At least he'd assured her he was coming home for Christmas. Whether he was prepared to take up his inheritance was another thing.

When she'd first arrived here, tired and tense, it had seemed a good idea to keep her mind blank if she was going to get any benefit from the holiday. All her agonizing wouldn't change a thing. There was absolutely nothing she could do about Sonia's overdependence on Curt, much less the dramatic shift in their relationship. It didn't meet with

her approval but she couldn't expect them to care about
that. She had to live *her* life—if she only knew what that was
to be. Things would have been very different had her own
mother lived. She was determined to track down the portrait Curt had mentioned. Sonia had denied all knowledge
of it.

The morning before she was due to fly home, Rachael was
lying peacefully on her beach towel in front of the house
when a long shadow fell across her, blocking the sun. A
flower, a creamy frangipani, dropped onto her breast, the
rich perfume assailing her senses. She sat up swiftly,
clutching her bikini top to her. Thinking herself alone, as
well she might, she had undone it to sunbathe.

Curt stood above her, smiling that smile of his that
weakened her knees. "So this is how you spend your time?"

"Curt! Where in the world did you come from?" The soft
balmy air was suddenly charged with energy, danger, the
excitement he carried about with him.

"Oh, come on. Surely you expected to see me?"

"On the contrary," she breathed. "I pictured you on the
job at Carrara."

"You've been thinking of me, then?" He lowered himself to the sand beside her, his rangy body clad in a casual
cotton shirt and beige slacks.

"Every night. I thought it appropriate to include you in
my nightly prayers."

"That's very nice of you. Much more than I expected."
The golden eyes moved over her, slowly, appraisingly. "This
holiday has done you a power of good. You look absolutely delectable. Full of sparkle."

"It's been perfect. Courtesy of you."

"Hello, Rachael," he said.

"Hello, Curt." *You Devil,* she thought. *Why do you always catch me when I'm at a disadvantage?*

"Want a hand with that?"

"You know damned well I don't." Somehow she managed to retie the bikini top, right there in front of him. She felt self-conscious now because she was showing so much of her body.

"You look beautiful."

"I look hot and flustered and well you know it."

He laughed and leaned back. "I wanted to surprise you. It seems I have."

She raised a hand in a vain effort to smooth back her unruly hair. "Would you mind passing me my cover-up?"

"For God's sake, why?" He spoke in an amused tone.

"I'm shy."

"Shy? When you've known me all your life?"

She shrugged a delicate shoulder. "There it is. These days you put me in mind of a lion about to pounce."

"On you?"

"You know darn well you scare me to death."

"Stop it, Rachael," he said in his beguiling voice. "Relax. I promise I'll keep my hands to myself."

"My beach coat, please."

"This doesn't sound like Rachael Munro, this scared little rabbit." Nevertheless he passed the cover-up to her and Rachael slipped into it, a filmy swirl of blues and greens.

"How have you been?" she asked.

"Fine." He eased back onto the sand, borrowing her cushion for his head. "No rain yet, as I'm sure you know. We just keep hoping, praying. Sonia enjoyed the party I gave for Philip and Natalie. Did she tell you?"

"I haven't spoken to her."

"You're a pair. You really are."

"It's the way she wanted it," Rachael replied, a little wounded. "I've spoken to Scott. I asked him up last weekend, but at the last minute he cried off. You know Scott. If a more interesting invitation comes along, he never can decline it. At least he's coming home for Christmas. He knows Sonia's desperate to see him.''

''He's got that right!''

''Sonia can be very possessive, Curt. Scotty doesn't like being fussed over. He'll probably bring one of his University friends to liven things up.''

''Then be prepared for extra work. Here, lie down beside me.'' He stretched lazily like a big cat. ''Marie tells me you haven't been out much at night.''

''There seem to be a lot of guys around here who want to pick me up,'' Rachael said wryly.

''*What?*''

''Don't worry, I haven't felt in the least romantic.''

''Then we'll have to change that.'' He put out a hand and stroked her cheek. ''In fact, we'll have dinner somewhere.''

''I'm not ready for your lessons in lovemaking, Curt.''

''Lessons? You're the limit, Rachael. You don't need them.'' He sat up abruptly in one lithe movement. ''Miss me?'' The golden eyes stared down into her flushed face.

''No.''

Quite casually he began to move his hand down the slope of her bare shoulder to her arm. ''Really?''

''Oh, just a little bit.''

''You're trembling.''

''You have that effect on me.''

''Quite a responsibility, Rachael.''

The big beautiful world narrowed to just the two of them. ''I always knew you'd influence my life.''

''But you think I'm just playing with you?'' Very gently he pushed a long lock of hair behind her ear.

''Maybe, Curt Carradine, you're just being yourself.''

''Which just goes to prove you don't know me at all.'' He leaned over her and dropped a brief hard kiss on her mouth.

LUNCH, AL FRESCO, on the deck. Freshly caught Queensland mud crab and salad. Afterward they went for a long walk along the beach, the sea gulls wheeling and dive-bombing the waves for fish. They surfed on and off until the mauve dusk, reveling in their own prowess and the crystal-line surf. It was a wonderful opportunity for Rachael to observe Curt relaxing. He was the perfect companion. It struck her that they had a great deal in common. They both worshiped nature. They were very active, athletic people. There was ease in their long association and shared inter-ests. With the subject of Miriwin not introduced, there was no strain in talking. They went from topic to topic, enjoy-ing their exchanges. It seemed neither of them wanted any part of conflict.

The restaurant Curt chose was the one Rachael had most admired. It was situated on the beach, the atmosphere very tropical and romantic. The rattan chairs that surrounded the glass-topped tables were plushly upholstered in a pale-blue fabric with a beach-inspired design of colorful little fish and ornamental seashells. Each table glowed with yellow table-cloths and napkins, and a squat yellow candle was adorned at the base with a halo of white butterfly orchids. It was heavenly. Ideal for lovers.

Curt was greeted enthusiastically and shown to a table that overlooked the lily pool and gardens with the ocean beyond. They took their time studying the menu. There were so many delicious things to have, and the restaurant was re-nowned for its seafood.

"What's it to be, Rose Red?" Curt asked indulgently, his glance resting lightly, shimmeringly, on her bare arms and throat. Tonight she was wearing a very pretty dress from the resort boutique, white for a summer night with a soft, sin-uous shape.

"The whole menu," she said smiling.

His golden gaze softened. "Have what you like."

"Well, maybe just parts of it." His glance on her was as powerful as body contact. She felt tremendously happy and full of energy.

In the end they ate wonderful local oysters and prawn tempura, red emperor fillets with capers and lemon, a platter of garden-fresh vegetables, all of it accompanied by a crisp chardonnay.

"Do you think you can manage anything else?" Curt teased.

"You're trying to ruin my figure."

"I must tell you the truth. Your body is beautiful. When you move it's nearly impossible for a man to take his eyes off you."

A hot desire brushed her, coloring her skin. "I thought you told Sonia I was a bit on the lanky side?"

"A ridiculous remark. The fortnight has done wonders. It gives me great pleasure to see you looking so well."

He sounded as though he really meant it. Touched and unsettled, Rachael leaned forward to caress a dazzling white petal of the orchid, her face luminous in the candlelight. "It's been so perfect. I hope this day never ends." In that moment she realized she was madly in love with him. Not the adolescent crush of earlier years, but a serious, heart-wrenching obsession that might never leave her.

They danced several times. Slow dances, and Curt held her close. They moved effortlessly together, their bodies completely in tune. It had taken a long time for her full sensuality to be revealed to her, but now that Curt had awakened her, her body might have been electrified. Ripple upon ripple of sensation moved through her in sparkling coils. Maybe the wine had made her reckless.

Rachael knew that when she awoke in the morning, it would all be over.

But it wasn't over yet. They went for a drive along the coast road. Almost in silence, as though being together was enough. From time to time, Rachael glanced away from the densely star-spangled sky to look at Curt's profile. It was strong, handsome, marvelously cut. Eventually he stopped the car near a downward curving path to the beach. It was a ravishing night, the sensuous swish of the breeze laden with freshness and salt. Comfortable beach houses stood back from the beach, light streaming out of huge picture windows onto the yellow daisy-laced dunes.

"No need for shoes," Curt said. "Leave them in the car."

The scented darkness enclosed them like a cloak. It created an intimacy that made her dizzy. From the trees a night bird's whistle pierced the air so exquisitely it filled Rachael with an intense yearning. A little frightened, she took off like a child, running headlong down the warm sandy slope. For years she had wanted something like this to happen. Now she was filled with such torrents of emotion she doubted she could handle it.

"Don't get too far ahead of me," Curt called.

That brought back memories of her childhood when he and his father had visited and Curt had been given the job of looking after her. He had taken his responsibilities very seriously. Even then.

When he reached her, he gave her a slow, disturbing smile as though acknowledging the summers of long ago. He took her hand. Folded it in his. The same bird was calling, its song affecting her more deeply now. Her blood had turned molten.

They walked in a fraught silence for a long time. It was the most physical experience Rachael had ever known. She was disarmed by the ardency of her own nature. It even seemed to her that at some level they were having a wordless conversation. There was an exhilaration in being there with him, her hand in his, skin on skin. It was like having a burst of stars inside her. Extravagant, but true.

Curt put his hands to her narrow waist, stopping her midstep. "Could this be the same fiery Rachael?"

She looked up at him, in thrall. "Don't spoil it. In a few hours we could be back to fighting."

The silver crescent moon etched out his strong features. "The worst part is, I can see that." He drew her to him, his arms enveloping her. "You're positive you *want* to fight?"

"Maybe there's no stopping it," she whispered.

"Except for *this*!"

He kissed her until her mind reeled and her heart fluttered like a caged bird inside her ribs. She had to cling to him for support. If this was moonlight madness, she never wanted it to end. At long, long last Curt was treating her like a woman, and a beautiful one at that.

THEY TOUCHED DOWN on Miriwin the following afternoon after the smoothest of flights. Matt was on hand to greet them. He looked tired and worn, but his face lit up as Rachael ran to greet him.

"Hiya, partner!" She kissed him.

"Hiya, partner, yourself! Don't you look beautiful!" He stood back, slapping his thigh. "Like a million dollars. And you've done somethin' to your hair. We've sure missed you around the place. Hi there, Curt!" The two men shook hands. "I expect you're stayin' for a cup of tea?"

Curt nodded amiably.

"Mighty fine of you to pick up Rachael." Sighing and heaving, he took hold of Rachael's two pieces of luggage.

"Hell, Matt, you sound like a Wurlitzer!" Smoothly Curt took the luggage from him. "Maybe you should have an orthopedic specialist take another look at that leg."

"Several have."

"Not for years, Matt," Rachael said anxiously. "He won't discuss this, Curt."

"You *want* me to have this leg off, girl?" Matt got behind the wheel of the Jeep.

"It might happen if you don't do something about it," Curt pointed out bluntly. "If you find out when the orthopedics specialist is there, I'll fly you in to Base Hospital."

Matt sighed. "Damn thing has been givin' me jip. Wyn never lets up. Not *your* leg, I tell her."

"Your fears might be groundless, Matt," Curt said quickly, "but I think it's reached the stage where you can't afford to delay."

Stubborn and argumentative with the women, Wyn and Rachael, Matt was surprisingly meek with Curt. "I'll get onto it this week."

Rachael glanced toward Curt, her face full of gratitude. On the short trip to the homestead they talked about the continuing effect of the drought. A tropical depression in the North had raised hopes, but it had shed only a little rain on the coast before weakening and heading back to sea. Rachael wanted to ask Matt up for a cup of tea, but she knew she'd only embarrass him. Sonia liked to keep a sharp dividing line between family and employees, choosing to ignore Rachael's deep affection for Matt and Wyn.

She greeted them on the veranda, blond and gleaming. In the first few moments she stared at Rachael as though she was a stranger.

"Well, what have you been doing to yourself?" she finally asked.

Rachael laughed and touched her hair. "You mean this? Cut, layered, treated. Money well spent. The hairdresser refused point-blank to cut off more than a couple of inches. He was quite taken with my hair."

"The outfit's new?" Sonia was still looking at Rachael in some surprise. Rachael was wearing a white silk singlet with white linen cuffed shorts and a colorful belt around her narrow waist, one of several brand-new purchases. The pure white set off her pale gold tan and her brilliant coloring. This was Rachael, the new woman, and one would have been forgiven for thinking Sonia didn't like it.

"She looks well, doesn't she?" Curt turned to Sonia casually.

"Fantastic!" Sonia agreed just at the right moment. "There was room for improvement, of course."

A few minutes later, Wyn wheeled the tea trolley out onto the veranda, and Rachael jumped up to kiss her, a gesture that was plainly annoying to Sonia.

"You look wonderful, love," Wyn whispered, remarkably adept when it came to all the little nuances. "We'll have a chat later."

Gradually Sonia seemed less unsettled as Curt asked her how she'd been sleeping.

"I can't give up the sleeping pills," she confessed in a soft voice, "but at least I'm down to one."

A day in the saddle might help, Rachael thought but wisely didn't say. She would have to make renewed efforts to get on with Sonia.

"I must say you look much better for your holiday," she told Rachael after Curt had gone. "Did you know Curt was coming for you?" This was said in an odd, challenging way.

"No idea. It came as the greatest surprise."

"And what's the beach house like? Marvelous, I suppose?"

"You'd love it. It sits on top of a headland looking out over the ocean. Not hard to take."

"So what did you do when he arrived?" Sonia asked with a playfulness that might have disguised a sharp jealousy.

Rachael pushed back in her chair, feigning drowsiness. "Oh, we went for a walk. Had a swim. I hadn't been out at night, so Curt took me to a restaurant. The seafood was divine."

"Did you have much to drink?"

"Surely you're not having visions of me under the table? One or two glasses of wine is my limit."

Sonia glanced down at her beautifully manicured hands. "He's certainly been kind to you. He obviously felt sorry for you. He told me himself he didn't think you had much capacity for enjoying yourself."

"He couldn't have said *that*, Sonia," Rachael snapped. She was fed up with the way Sonia twisted remarks.

"I'm telling you he did," Sonia said coolly. "It was at the party he gave for his cousin Philip and his wife. I had a marvellous time, by the way. She's a rather plain little thing, and Philip is so handsome. A mystery to me how they got together. I suppose she's clever. A barrister, I believe."

"That would make her clever," Rachael said in a measured voice.

Sonia scarcely heard her, busy giving a detailed account of what she wore. Clothes were extremely important to Sonia. Rachael learned she had dazzled everyone in her silver-and-turquoise short evening dress with the diamond-and-pearl earrings and matching bracelet that "Alec bought me on our last trip to Hong Kong."

Rachael only just avoided shaking her head. Curt had been very attentive, Sonia was telling her. So was a man called Anthony Fallon. Mellyn. Something like that.

"Curt put me in the guest suite with that exquisite Chinese wallpaper. Dozens of pink roses in my room. My favorites. We all took our time at breakfast, then Curt drove us around the property. I sat up front with him. I think his cousin was very impressed with me. That's important."

Rachael sighed.

WYN WAS SITTING at the kitchen table enjoying a quiet cup of tea when Rachael walked in.

"It's lovely to have you home!" Wyn breathed. "Without you, your stepma and I really don't get on. She's become very critical of everything I do."

Rachael's expression saddened and she dropped a kiss on Wyn's head. "You're the best, Wyn. The best of 'em all. That includes Curt's latest housekeeper."

"Yeah, I reckon that, too," Wyn agreed dryly. "I'm willin' to bet she won't last long. Of course, Heather Craig was a marvel, but she had to retire sometime. That was really something, Curt flying to the coast to bring you home."

"I'm sure he combined it with other business."

"Well, tell me how it went," Wyn urged. "It's so dreary when you're not about."

Rachael pulled up a chair and spoke at length while Wyn listened with interest. "Scotty was supposed to come one weekend, but at the last minute he backed out."

"Sounds like Scotty," Wyn grunted. "He's coming home for Christmas, I hope?"

"He promised me faithfully."

"His mother will be pleased. She lives for that boy. Yet that's one of the reasons Scotty stays away. His mother has such a possessive streak."

"Scotty's her only child. Anyway, I'm glad she had a nice time at Curt's."

"Yes, she told me." Wyn peered down at the brown spots on her hands. "I think *she* thinks he's developing a romantic interest in her."

"I thought so myself," Rachael muttered, but for once Wyn didn't catch on.

"Nonsense!" Wyn said flatly. "I know your stepma is a good-looking woman, but she's nearly forty. Why, Curt's just past thirty."

"Thirty-one. He had a birthday in August. Wouldn't you know it. The definitive Leo."

"*You* could get him if you tried," Wyn suddenly burst out.

"My dear Wyn. I'm a commoner. He's a prince," Rachael teased.

"I'm telling you, you could," Wyn insisted.

"I don't think so, Wyn. Many others have tried. At least he realizes I'm no longer a kid."

"He liked you when you were a kid, too. I remember him calling you a 'spunky little thing' and 'magic with the horses.' You could only have been around ten."

"I remember." Rachael smiled gently.

"Just watch out for your stepma," Wyn warned. "That coolness of hers is only a smokescreen. She's one tough, determined lady."

SCOTT ARRIVED HOME four days later with Aussie super-model Elle McPherson's look-alike in tow. Rachael, who had taken the Jeep down to the airstrip to meet her brother, watched in fascination as Scott and a female companion alighted from the freight plane and came toward her, all smiles, arms entwined. They were two beautiful young people walking into the sun. Sonia would be upset, Rachael thought with immediate dismay. Sonia loathed surprise visits at the best of times, but a male companion was tolerated. The arrival of a *girlfriend* would not be well received.

Scott bounded toward Rachael and wound his arms around her, giving her a big hug. "Hey, hey, you're looking terrific! It's great to see you, Rae." From his vantage point of six two, he bent to kiss her. Golden Scott, dressed in trendy designer gear, not classically handsome but so alive and attractive, with Rachael's brand of unselfconscious sex appeal. "Meet Midge. Midge Cawley." He put out a long arm and dragged Midge forward.

It took Rachael less than thirty seconds to decide she liked Midge. Scott and Midge were currently madly in love. Midge, almost as ravishing as Elle, stood five eleven in her flats, with a waterfall of dead-straight, shiny brown hair, sparkling brown eyes, a wholesome, attractive face and a body that could have adorned *Sports Illustrated*. The two young women shook hands, decided they liked one another, and spontaneously exchanged quick kisses.

"It's great to meet you, Rachael. Scotty's told me so much about you but he didn't say you're gorgeous. Not even that you had *beautiful* red hair. I thought you'd be blond like him," Midge chattered on, "but you're not alike at all. Say, this is a marvelous place," she added, her eyes alight with wonder and speculation. "You must own half of Australia!"

"Midge knows nothing about the outback." Scott looked down at Midge fondly. "She found the trip mind-boggling. If you want to see a real cattle station, you'll have to meet our neighbor, Curt Carradine. You could drive through three states and never be off his land."

"Wow! Isn't that incredible!" Midge looked so thrilled Rachael thought she was about to break into a tap dance. "My real name's Michelle, by the way. That went out the door when I started to grow. My brother thought of it. You know, giving me a name that's the opposite of how I look. Isn't that vile? No one, but no one, calls me Michelle."

"Still, Midge suits you." Rachael smiled. "You could easily be a model."

"Her sister is!" Scott said proudly, dropping a kiss on the top of Midge's shiny head.

"Nicole's been living in New York for the past two years," Midge explained. "She made it almost as soon as she arrived. She's a real stunner. *Bellissima!* She wants me to join her if I can ever move away from Mum and Dad. I sent over a portfolio just for fun, and Nickie showed it around. Her agency is interested."

"That's exciting news, Midge," Rachael said, feeling inexplicably relieved. "Life in the Big Apple."

Midge looked doubtful. "Of course I wouldn't go unless—"

"Unless what?" Rachael asked swiftly as Scott appeared to apply pressure to Midge's arm.

Midge gave Scott a perplexed look. "I was going to say unless Scotty comes with me. We could have crazy times together. Say, what's the matter with you, Scott? That hurt!"

Rachael couldn't mask her shock. "*You* want to go to New York, Scott?"

Midge beamed, showing engaging dimples. "Scotty sent a portfolio, as well. He photographs like you wouldn't believe! He's so darn sexy. Nickie thought he had great potential. You can earn big bucks if you hit the big time. Nickie's been on location all over the world. She's even..."

Rachael tuned out Midge's chatter. *Well, I'll be damned,* she thought. She had the oddest impression her whole world was turning upside down.

"You look surprised, Rachael," Midge offered hesitantly.

"I am a bit," Rachael admitted. "There's never a dull moment around here. Anyway, welcome to Miriwin, Midge. I do hope you'll enjoy your stay."

"Oh, I will!" Midge's expression brightened. "Scotty's promised he'll teach me to ride a horse. There's a big swimming pool, too, isn't there? And a great house! I can't wait to meet Scotty's mother. I sure hope she likes me."

Rachael almost advised her to keep her fingers crossed. Under cover of loading the Jeep with station supplies and Midge's luggage, Rachael managed a few private words with her brother.

"Don't say anything about New York to Sonia, Scotty. Right now, I think it would kill her."

Scott's blue eyes fired. "Keepin' things from Mum! I hate it. But I have to do it all the time. You know I want to travel, Rae. I only have one life. Do I have to live it Mum's way?"

"Listen, Scotty, you don't put yourself out for anybody," Rachael said wryly. "Can't you spare her a year or two?"

"I'm here, aren't I?" Scott flushed. "I just hate being tied down. I hate having things expected of me. Come to that, I hate responsibility. Too much pressure. A man can take it up in his thirties. Not now."

"And what about Midge? Could she get hurt?"

Scott's expression softened. "I'm mad about her, Rae."

"For how long?" Rachael didn't even hate herself for asking it.

"None of your business, Rae."

"Maybe." Rachael shrugged. "You should have confirmed you were bringing a friend. A girlfriend, at that. Just common courtesy! It's not fair to Midge, either."

"Aw, come off it, Rae," Scott groaned. "You know perfectly well Mum doesn't want me to bring girls."

There was nothing Rachael could say to that. She knew it was the truth.

THE BRILLIANT SMILE died on Sonia's face as her eyes took in the occupants of the Jeep. She stood clutching the railing, and Scott rolled his eyes in his sister's direction. "See what I mean?"

"You bet. Race up and say hello."

Alarm bells appeared to be ringing in Midge's head. "Everything's okay, isn't it?" she asked uncertainly.

"Of course!" Rachael gave her a warm smile. "Scotty forgot to say you were coming, but you're most welcome. Come up and meet Sonia."

Midge seemed rooted to the ground. For a minute Rachael expected her to say, "No way!"

"That's Scotty's *mother?*" she finally asked, sounding puzzled.

"Yes, that's Sonia. She looks tiny beside Scotty, doesn't she?"

"She doesn't look like *anyone's* mother," Midge said almost desperately. "I had no idea she was so young and... and glamorous."

"Oh, yes, Sonia is *very* glamorous. But no need to be frightened of her, Midge. She's very nice. Here, let me open the door."

Midge stared at her. "Scotty didn't prepare me for any of you. Or this place! A huge mansion—tucked away in the bush."

"They built them that way in the old days, Midge," Rachael said hastily. "You won't have any trouble finding your way around. Let's go up. Scotty's calling us."

When confronted by Midge towering so sweetly over her, Sonia made a commendable effort to be gracious, but all three young people were uncomfortably aware that she was quietly simmering underneath. Scotty rescued Midge on the pretext of showing her the house and as they walked away,

Midge with widened eyes, Sonia gestured for Rachael to remain.

"You knew about this, didn't you?" Sonia asked hotly.

"Please Sonia, keep your voice down!" Rachael looked anxiously toward the main reception rooms.

"Kindly answer my question."

"Lord, Sonia, what's this all about? I don't *really* know anything, I swear."

"What on earth is that girl doing here?"

"She's Scott's friend."

"Friend!" Sonia said scathingly. She seemed to swallow some lump in her throat.

"Please don't make her feel bad, Sonia," Rachael begged. "She was so looking forward to meeting you."

"*I* was so looking forward to having Scott to myself. Is that so unusual?" Sonia seemed in danger of bursting into tears. "Is that too much to ask?"

"I understand, Sonia. I know what Scotty means to you."

"How could you? You haven't had a child!" Sonia's blue eyes were bereft. "I feel so *alone,* Rachael."

"But you're not! I'll do everything I can to help you, and Scotty *has* come home. He loves you, Sonia, but he has to have a girlfriend. Keep in mind that if you're cool to Midge he might leave again. He's got a place to go, after all. Dad did buy him that apartment in Brisbane—so he wouldn't have to rough it on campus."

"Doesn't that girl know how I've suffered?" Sonia asked. "Of course she would have no idea about depression."

"Who knows what's happened in *her* life, Sonia? Let's get to know her. Give her a chance."

"She's so *big!*"

"Sonia, she's stunning. Things will be very difficult if we're not pleasant to her."

"I truly believe I couldn't stand it, except for Curt," Sonia said. "I wanted to bring him and Scotty closer together. There's so much we have to talk about. Now this girl has turned up."

"I don't think Curt and Scotty are ever going to be chums," Rachael said shortly. "There's a huge gulf between them. And what do you mean by having so much to talk about?"

Sonia looked at her blankly. "How can we possibly talk about anything with a complete stranger around?"

"Scotty's in love with her."

"Nonsense!" Sonia fiercely rejected the idea. "He'll believe himself in love a dozen times before he gets married. In any case, I couldn't countenance that girl. She's very ordinary and she's too tall altogether. I have an entirely different type of girl in mind. One whose mouth doesn't fall open when she looks around a large house."

"Say that to Scotty, Sonia, and there might only be the two of us for Christmas."

"Who are you to lecture me?" Sonia demanded. "I'm absolutely devoted to my son, and he is to me. All *you* can worry about is what's going to happen to Miriwin. Scotty might want to get rid of it for all you know."

"And he might not," Rachael retorted. "Owning a station like Miriwin gives one social status. Scott's always liked that."

"Well, it's not as though he has to *stay* here! There are such things as managers, and very good ones, too. Curt knows them all."

"Then you've discussed it?" Anger and disillusionment sounded in Rachael's voice.

Sonia looked intensely irritated. "Silly girl, of course! What are you so horribly hurt about? Curt and I are... special friends."

"If he's been colluding with you behind my back, he's certainly no friend to me."

"Oh, do stop, Rachael," Sonia said in agitation. "You're not the only one around here to be considered. There are so many things we have to work out during these holidays. That's why I'm disappointed that girl's here."

WYN AND RACHAEL hastily prepared Midge's room. "I don't mean to sound picky, but I've never heard a lass go on and on so much about nothing." Wyn sighed.

"She's excited, Wyn." Rachael tucked a pillow into its boronia-scented case. "And she's madly in love."

"Oh, oh, oh," Wyn said. "Your stepma's not about to compete with anyone for Scott."

"Scotty should have told her he was bringing Midge."

"He should have told us *all,*" Wyn remarked dryly. "But that's Scott. He's never in his short life thought of anyone but himself. Could be hereditary, of course."

"Do you want to hear a secret?" Rachael sat down on the bed, looking hard at Wyn.

Wyn glanced up, dismay on her face. "You're not going to tell me Scotty's engaged or married? Something like that? I keep remembering how impulsive he is."

"No." Rachael shook her head. "I don't think Scotty will go into marriage quickly. You heard Midge say her sister is a model in New York?"

"Roughly a dozen times."

"Well, Midge wants to join her and—wait for it—take Scotty. They sent portfolios, which apparently went over very well. Scotty was always marvelously photogenic."

Wyn looked flabbergasted. "So he's movin' out as soon as he moves in?"

"I would say very probably."

Wyn fell into a velvet-upholstered armchair. "It's all I can do to take this in. Scotty wants to be a male model. His father would turn in his grave."

"He sure would," Rachael said with real feeling.

"His mother will faint when she hears it."

"She'll be devastated," Rachael agreed. "It's not as though Scotty was thinking of it as a career, though. He just wants to be with Midge and have a lot of fun."

"So what happens if Midge makes it big, like the sister?"

"Ah," Rachael breathed. "Who knows what crazy things might happen? It's getting to be like a soap opera around here."

YET MIDGE PROVED the easiest possible guest. Not that anyone other than Scott saw a lot of her. The two of them disappeared for hours on end, returning in such high spirits it infected them all. Except Sonia... Rachael thought they were as endearing and carefree as puppies. Sonia complained privately that she was going out of her mind with Midge's incessant giggling. Sonia's moods tended to seesaw between seething and self-pity.

Curt invited them all to a weekend polo match on Carrara, but Rachael, still gnawed by suspicion, decided not to go. Scott and Midge seemed genuinely disappointed; Sonia took it in her stride.

Saturday morning she stood by the foyer mirror, turning sideways to admire her outfit, slim tapered pants of Wedgwood-blue linen and a silver-embroidered matching shirt. "Do you think I should have bangs cut?" she asked Rachael. "I saw a short, feathery style in a magazine I quite liked."

"I'm sure you could wear them," Rachael answered, earning one of Sonia's rare smiles.

"And what are you going to do with yourself?" Sonia picked up her chic shoulder bag.

"Order in some more supplies. Machine parts, fuel, stuff like that."

Scott and Midge joined them in the hall a few minutes later, looking extraordinarily attractive. Both were wearing casual shirts and tight-fitting jeans. Their long-limbed bodies were so lithe and elegant, Rachael could well see how they might make their mark as fashion models. Scotty had obviously spoken to Midge, because not one word had been breathed about their proposed trip to New York. Rachael got the impression Midge was terrified of holding a conversation with Sonia at all.

Rachael drove them down to the airstrip, arriving just as Curt was touching down. She expected she'd only have to wave them off, but Curt had other ideas. As soon as his passengers were seated, he made a beeline for Rachael.

"I hadn't reckoned on your not coming." He looked at her in surprise. "You enjoy a good match, and it promises to be one."

She flushed under his brilliant gaze. "This is a working station, remember? I spend time in the office seven days a week."

"Isn't Scott helping out?" Curt's black brows drew together.

"Scotty is entertaining Midge."

He made a disgusted sound. "You're just making a martyr of yourself, Rachael."

"I'm not asking for your sympathy."

"And you certainly won't get it. Obviously you're not going to tell me what's bothering you."

"I'm just realizing how little I know you," she flashed at him.

"I'm sorry to hear that." His tone was marked with danger signals. "Could it be that something *else* has been said?"

Hot color stained her cheeks. "I'm incensed that you and Sonia have been discussing a possible manager for Miriwin."

"Really?" he said abruptly. "You know, I think you'll have to decide at some point whether you trust me."

"Are you saying it's *not* true?"

"You *want* to believe it, don't you? This is all starting to get thick with intrigue, and intrigue isn't my style. Sonia brought the subject up only the other day. Nothing shocking about it. It's a possibility that has to be faced. She asked for my opinion and I gave it. In no way does it suggest a possible sale of Miriwin. Take some advice, Rachael. Don't go insulting me to my face."

Rachael struggled for self-control. "And don't go discussing Miriwin's future behind my back."

"Feeling as you do, why didn't you contest the will?" he erupted, his expression ominous. "You can't have it all ways. Your father left the property to Scott. If you want to pick on anyone, pick on your brother."

"Thank you, I will."

"And next time, have a thought before you go accusing me of anything. Besides, you're so paranoid on the subject you might have misinterpreted what Sonia said."

Rachael's eyes sparked. A relentless pressure was building up inside her. "You're very fast to align yourself with Sonia. I am *not* lying or exaggerating."

He raised his handsome head and stared into the distance. "Then it's possible Sonia wants to score off you." He laughed. A harsh sound, without humor. "You're a big girl now. Try to figure it out."

CHAPTER FIVE

RACHAEL SPENT a miserable day mulling over her confrontation with Curt. She had caught his repugnance, and it had affected her. What had he meant about Sonia's wanting to score off her? By deliberately lying? To Rachael, who loathed duplicity, it seemed incomprehensible. Was Sonia trying to rattle her and thus keep the upper hand? She'd had it for so long, controlling and directing Rachael's behavior since she'd been little more than a baby. Even Wyn had taken to warning her to watch out for Sonia.

So why couldn't she accept what Curt had told her? He claimed to have no designs on Miriwin, claimed not to be colluding with Sonia. No one had ever accused him of being dishonest. Except her. That she'd done so now took her breath away. One thing was certain. Underneath, all the old tensions were still in place and Miriwin was at the center of them.

In the evening the family arrived home. Midge's shoulder bag was packed with dozens of instant photographs she'd taken. She and Scott were full of their day, coming into the library to join Rachael, but Sonia had swept through the house like a small cyclone, complaining she had a violent headache.

"She could, too," Scott told Rachael after Midge had gone off to shower and change for dinner.

"Something happened. I could tell."

"Is it possible Mum's struck on Curt?" Scott asked abruptly, bewilderment on his face.

"If she was, I could understand it. Let's face it, he's a thrilling kind of man."

"But she's only just lost Dad!"

"Those were my thoughts, Scotty, but Sonia tells me she has no time to waste."

"Good God!" Scott breathed. "I wouldn't have thought it possible. Not that Mum doesn't look terrific. She's a very glamorous lady. But Curt!"

"You look shocked."

"Aren't you? Hell, Curt can have anyone he wants. And he'd want kids, too. Mum's nearly forty—and she's not a huge success as mothers go."

"Forty is okay these days to have kids."

"Oh, turn it up, Rae," Scott said in disgust. "Andrée Haddon was there today. She presented Curt with the trophy and managed to get in quite a kiss. I thought Mum was going to take a swing at her. She was hopeless at hiding her feelings, and you know how good she usually is at that. Did you know about any of this?"

Rachael fixed her eyes on one of the paintings on the wall, and shrugged lightly, "Not when it first happened—and right under my nose, too. I know now, of course."

"Makes you wonder, doesn't it, if Mum ever loved Dad?"

"That, Scotty, is beyond my frail understanding."

SONIA DIDN'T APPEAR again that evening, and the next morning Rachael went down to the yards where the men were working hard to get the cattle on the giant road trains. It didn't take her long to realize Matt was far from well. She took his arm, pulling him to one side.

"You must rest now, Matt. I insist."

"I'm like you, sweetheart. I don't know when to quit."

"So that's why I've decided I'm the boss today. Paddy?" She turned her head, calling their best hand. "Take over, will you?"

"Sure thing, Miss Rachael." Paddy sketched a brief salute and went deep into the milling throng.

"Where's that brother of yours, Rae?" Matt grunted.

"I wish I could tell you. He and Midge took off around seven. I think they had plans to see the cave drawings."

Matt shook his head. "It just doesn't occur to him to work."

"Work *is* a problem."

"And your stepma doesn't rein him in."

"It's hard, Matt, when she can't find him. She's up against a little thing called being in love."

Matt looked at her quickly. "Scotty?"

Rachael smiled. "Anything's possible. Let's forget Scotty for now. The orthopedic surgeon will be at Base Hospital all next week. Curt has offered to fly you in. That means you're going, if Wyn and I have to tie you up."

Matt scratched at a thick eyebrow distractedly. "You realize this could be the beginning of the end, Rae."

"Don't say such a thing!" Rachael was upset and unnerved. "You're jumping to conclusions, Matt. Only the doctor can find out exactly what's wrong. I don't have to tell you you'll always have a place here."

"If it was up to you," Matt said miserably. "That's somethin' you and me have to talk about. I just know in my bones Scotty isn't gonna stay. And that Midge! She's not gonna want to live out here. She's a city girl if ever I saw one. She's only havin' fun."

Rachael, sadly, could not deny it.

IN LATE AFTERNOON, while the station watched with bated breath, great thunderclouds built up, towering castles that nevertheless yielded not one drop of rain. The next morning they learned tropical Cyclone Lena was heading toward the coast from the Coral Sea. By afternoon, Cape York and the Gulf country were receiving a long-awaited deluge.

The suffering outback went ecstatic. On the stations and in the outback towns perfectly ordinary people were seen to drop to their knees, imploring the Lord to keep up the good work. The aborigines, interpreting the sound of thunder as the voice of the Great Spirit, intensified their ceremonies. The movements and patterns of the clouds, too, were of great importance. Jacky Eaglehawk reported millions of strange little birds at the river. These were taken as heralds used by the Great Spirit.

Within days, the Top End was experiencing torrential rain. All along the Carradine chain that extended across Queensland into the Northern Territory, great winding rivers were rolling billions of gallons of water into a river system that spread southward into the drought-stricken areas. Managers were delirious with joy, and Curt relayed all advance information to his neighbors in the southwest. This was no ordinary occurrence. This was a renewal of life. If the miracle continued, the great river system of the Georgina, Diamantina and the Cooper could fill up. The dead Heart would turn back into the inland sea of prehistory, and every living thing would enter into celebration. The desert would spring into breathtaking life. The blood-red sands would be woven with countless millions of wildflowers, clear to the horizon—poppies and cattails, fire bush, hop bush, the exquisite cleomes, yellow and white paper daisies in the trillions, the scarlet desert pea, native lilies and hibiscus, ipomoeas and pink parakelia. No one who ever saw the desert gardens mantling the endless plains forgot the miracle of beauty and splendor.

On Miriwin and Carrara Downs, to the north and north-west, not one drop of rain had fallen. It was still the wait-ing, hoping, praying game. Curt flew in midweek, a few sharp edges around his formidable charm. Carrara Downs was the flagship of the Carradine empire, and it was suffer-ing just like everyone else.

Always vulnerable to him, the more so since their time together at the beach, Rachael felt as though a protective layer of skin had been stripped from her. As soon as she caught sight of him talking to Sonia out on the veranda, she was thrown into emotional turmoil. Sonia was laughing, her porcelain skin flushed. Being in love made a woman beau-tiful, Rachael observed almost dispassionately. She only prayed it would not bring her humiliation.

Midge and Scott returned in time for the ritual of after-noon tea, with Sonia seated prettily behind the elegant ster-ling silver tea service. Normally Midge kept very quiet in Sonia's presence, but Curt's arrival had her chattering mer-rily. Eyelids batted, dazzling dimples flashed, while Sonia's ice-blue eyes registered a few degrees below zero. She was far from pleased with being upstaged, but Midge didn't even give her a cursory glance.

Afterward Curt held Sonia's chair and thanked her for a delightful afternoon tea, and Rachael looked directly at him for the first time. She spoke crisply. "I wonder if you'd mind coming down to see Matt? He's at the bungalow, resting."

"What on earth for?" Sonia demanded. "Didn't you tell me the road trains were here?"

"They've been and gone," Rachael said. "Matt's leg is giving him hell. The sooner we get him into hospital the better."

"Poor old devil!" Scott was sympathetic. "That leg has never been right. If you're all okay here, Midge and I will go riding for an hour. When the sun starts to go down, the sky is spectacular."

Moments later, Rachael and Curt were moving through the home gardens in silence. They could see the red roof of Matt's and Wyn's bungalow through the trees up ahead. The leaves were shimmering in the heat sending down wisps of blossoms as the faintest breeze blew.

"You're very quiet," Curt said.

"I'm trying not to court trouble."

"Yes, you do seem to put your foot in it."

Rachael stopped and broke off spent gardenias along the stone wall. "Look, I'm sorry about the other day."

"For how long?" he asked ironically.

"It's hard for me to accept that Sonia would deliberately misrepresent your discussions."

"Much easier to accuse me of going behind your back?"

"Forgive me." Rachael looked away. "It's all tied up with the old days."

"Except that I'm a straight shooter. At least most people put me in that category."

"I've offended you, haven't I?" Rachael asked with urgency in her voice.

"Yes, ma'am, you have. I'm waiting for an apology."

"I did say I'm sorry. Give me another chance."

"Right!" His golden eyes glittered. "But let me tell you it's the only one you've got left."

Immediately her heart lightened and she glanced up at him with a quick smile. "I know." She felt the familiar sweetness and excitement gripping her tight.

He must have felt something, too, because his expression changed to unmistakable sensuality.

"Imagine Rachael without her smile! It's the most beautiful I've ever seen."

"Then why has it taken you all this time to tell me?"

"I just had to protect myself against it. Because one of my cardinal rules is not plucking babes from the cradle."

"You seem willing enough now."

He placed his finger on the tip of her small straight nose. "Who reminded me she was all of twenty-three?"

"You're only eight years older than me, you know."

"Ah, but, Rachael, I've lived a *lot* longer." He picked up her hand, holding it. "Is Matt expecting me?"

"No, but you can make him behave. There's something else you should know—Scott and Midge are planning to go to New York to work in the fashion industry."

"What?" Curt tightened his grip on her fingers in amazement. "How in the wide, wide world did this come about?"

"Sonia doesn't know yet," Rachael said, withdrawing her hand and flexing it. "You can imagine how she'll react."

"Like a firecracker." An unwilling amusement crept into his voice.

"Midge's sister is a top model there. They sent portfolios that went over very well."

"For cryin' out loud!" Curt groaned. "I'm beginning to wonder if you Munros are certifiable."

"Leave *me* out of it," Rachael said.

"Oh, come on," he said tauntingly. "So Scott wants to be a model?"

"It's just a bit of fun to him."

"You feel that's fair? With all the straightening out Miriwin needs?"

"Matt and I can do it if we work hard."

"Matt with the game leg? He's been knocking himself out for you."

"Don't I know it!" Rachael could feel her quick temper rise.

"For God's sake," Curt said quietly, "your father would turn in his grave."

"I'll admit he'd be shocked. To Dad, male models wouldn't be real men at all."

"I guess I'd prefer my son to do something else," Curt said in a mildly despairing tone. "How did your father ever come to believe Scott could take over the station?"

"Forgive me for saying it, but Sonia worked on him, and paternal pride did the rest. I guess Dad had some outdated beliefs about women."

"He certainly wasn't as enlightened as he should have been. Pardon me if I'm asking a stupid question, but have you told Scott how you feel about this?"

"I've tried to." Rachael shook her head. "Without much success...."

"You're as soft on him as the rest of them," Curt said. "By the sound of it, Scott's going to need another ten years to settle down. It's fairly obvious now he doesn't intend to take up his responsibilities."

"He's prepared to let me run the place."

Curt sounded disgusted. "He'd let you cut your own throat."

"That's not fair."

"Isn't it?" he asked cynically. "Then why is he hiding behind your skirts? Why doesn't he tell his mother what he intends to do? Surely she has a right to know."

"Scott doesn't like . . . unpleasantness."

"And not getting his own way. It doesn't bother him how hard *you* work."

Rachael caught the glint of real anger in his voice. "We'll work it out, Curt. Please don't take him to task over it."

"He needs a good talking to, Rachael. And that's the truth."

"Anyway, it mightn't happen. Not when Sonia has her say."

"Maybe you should all set up a meeting with your accountants," Curt suggested. "You know as well as I do the picture isn't as rosy as Sonia and Scott think. Miriwin's in bad shape. You're run off your feet. So's Matt. Paddy is an incredible worker, but he hasn't got a brain in his head. Who else is there?"

"No one. I agree. Does that make you happy?"

"None of it makes me happy, Rachael," Curt said soberly. "I love the land too much to see Miriwin falling to pieces. Your father made a few bad decisions in recent years. He should have checked out that machinery dealer—Dawson—but he didn't." He sighed. "I leaned over backward to try to help him."

"I know you did, Curt. Dad really appreciated it, but he was so stubborn. I told him Dawson was a con man myself."

"Maybe, Rachael, you should just sell the place."

"Never!" She tossed up her head.

"And what if it becomes impossible for you to hold on to it? Scott goes away, leaving you here. You get a manager in. What next? Even if you find a good one, you'll all have to work like dogs. I know you're a hard and willing worker, but you *are* a woman, which in this world means you have to push yourself that much harder. God, Rachael, you could get yourself killed. Cattle stations aren't fun parks. They can be downright dangerous, as we both know. If you don't want me to talk to him, you tell Scott to discuss his plans with his mother. Decisions have to be made."

"I will. I swear."

"These plans of Scott's change everything. Surely you see that?"

Rachael felt the tension running from Curt to her. "You're never going to take this away from us, Curt," she said urgently. Her eyes blurred with tears.

He looked down at her a little savagely, as though her tears unnerved him. "Rachael, things might get so bad the bank will wrench Miriwin out from under you."

She focused dazedly on his face. "Surely we're not in so deep. Dad kept such a lot to himself, but the accountants' report will be in soon."

"Then expect a few revelations." His shapely mouth went wry.

"Is there more about this I should know?"

He looked directly into her eyes. "Rachael, I'm only making assumptions based on what your father told me and my own experience running the chain. As I see it, the only way you can pull through is for Scott to knuckle down. He must be ready, willing and able to take up his inheritance. That's what it was all about. He never once said to his father, 'I don't want the job.'"

"In a way he was scared of Dad."

"I realize that." Curt nodded. "But he should have found the courage. I know he's young, but he has to find a goal in life, instead of drifting aimlessly, having a good time. Even then, you'd have to come up with extra capital and a good manager to replace Matt, who's coming to the end of his days as overseer. He'll have to be given a lighter job. He can't get away with the sort of backbreaking work he's been doing. More importantly, neither can you."

Rachael didn't respond. There was nothing she could say.

MATT WAS SO THRILLED to see Curt his weathered face turned beet-red.

"Come in, come in," he invited. "I was wonderin' how much longer I could take lyin' down. Rachael, honey, let's have a cup of tea." He nodded to her, beaming, and Rachael took herself off to the neat cozy kitchen where she listened unashamedly from behind the door.

The two men discussed the rains, how they were affecting the outback, the rising price of beef, until Curt introduced the subject of Matt's troublesome leg.

Knowing Matt so well, Rachael pressed the back of her hand to her mouth. Now was the time Matt would start protesting that the rest had done him a power of good.

He did no such thing. He listened quietly while Curt outlined a plan to fly him and Wyn into Base Hospital two days later, when the visiting orthopedic surgeon would be in attendance.

"I have to go," Matt said simply. "My dear lady wife has been givin' me hell, not to speak of this blue-eyed girl." He looked up as Rachael reentered the room. "Ever see her, Curt, when she's determined?"

"I'm scared witless by the thrust of her chin. But she means well by you, Matt. She thinks the world of you."

"She could have been our own child," Matt said briskly, to hide real emotion. "I took care of her outside the house. Wyn took care of her inside."

"That's a whole lot of taking care of," Rachael teased.

They stayed for another half hour, and Matt waved them off as they walked away from the bungalow. "I was prepared for an argument," Curt said with a satisfied smile, "but he was remarkably amenable to everything I said."

Rachael nodded. "I think it's reached that point. Thanks, Curt, for helping out."

When they returned to Miriwin, both realized there was no escaping dinner. It was set up in the formal dining room as was currently Sonia's wont, but Scott, like most males, wasn't all that keen on dining by candlelight. He turned on the chandeliers, clearly annoying his mother.

"I'll want to see what I'm eating, Mum."

"Why can't you see with the candles?"

"It's too damned gloomy for a start. Place looks much better with the chandeliers on, if you ask me. I'd better go dress. Curt should be down soon."

Rachael didn't intervene in this exchange, but walked upstairs to see Midge. She knocked on the door and Midge opened it immediately, looking straight from the catwalk in a strapless, red crepe dress that showed off her spectacular body to perfection.

"Wow!" Rachael breathed. "Where did you get that little number?"

"Nice, isn't it?" Midge smoothed the fabric over her hips. "Nickie sent it to me from New York. Take a look at the label," she urged. "Donna Karan."

"Poor old Scotty!" Rachael remarked. "Wait till he sees you."

"Damned right!" Midge said emphatically. "He's been waffling a bit about coming to New York."

Rachael walked past Midge, who was preening in front of the pier mirror, and sat in an armchair. "He's needed here, Midge. That must be worrying him. Scotty inherited Miriwin and all its responsibilities. Didn't he tell you that?"

"Of course he did!" Midge flashed her brilliant grin. "But surely he doesn't have to take over right now. Isn't he entitled to a little fun? I mean, it's not as though we're going to stay there."

"And what happens if your career takes off? Like your sister."

"I'm not a patch on Nickie," Midge said firmly. "I should have brought you some of her glossies. I'm sort of *fresh*. She's glamorous in a way I could never be. I'm not that ambitious, either. And I like to eat. We wouldn't stay in New York—it's more like an extended holiday. Scotty's not thrilled about modeling clothes or posing. He's too much the Aussie male. But he said he could put up with it, just to be with me in New York. At least that's what he said before we got here."

"And now?" Rachael asked with bated breath.

Midge shrugged. "He doesn't want to let you down. He says you've worked hard enough."

"That's heartening!" Rachael was pleasantly surprised. After a silence, she asked, "Would you ever want to live here, Midge?"

Midge's brown eyes grew serious. "I love the house. It's marvelous—the high ceilings and the size of the rooms. I grew up in an old brick-and-tile bungalow. And when I first met Scotty, I thought he was a prince. So tall and golden, with such a posh voice. You all speak like that. Gosh, I could listen to Curt all day long. That's a heart-stopping kind of voice. No wonder poor old Sonia can't control her tremors. Help, there I go again! I'm so thick!" Midge looked mortified. "I should just keep my mouth shut."

"What about the life-style, Midge?" Rachael persisted with her own line of thought. "The isolation?"

"That's a drag!" Midge caught her waterfall of hair and smoothed it. "I'm a city girl, but I guess I could change. Hell, let's forget it for tonight, Rae. I'm so excited. Having dinner in that dining room of yours is like being in the movies." She slipped an arm around Rachael's waist and they walked to the door.

Downstairs in the drawing room, Sonia appeared to be regaling Curt with an amusing story while they were nursing their pre-dinner drinks. Both looked up as Rachael and Midge entered the room, and Curt rose to his feet, his expression admiring.

"I'm surrounded by beauty tonight," he told them, a kind of challenge behind the sparkling look.

Midge blushed very sweetly and Rachael dropped a curtsy. "Why, thank you, Curt. It was our intention to dazzle you."

"Then let me confirm you've succeeded. You all look ravishing." He turned to include Sonia who drew her slight body up in the armchair.

"Good heavens, Rachael, where did you get that outfit?" she demanded in a faintly grudging voice.

Rachael raised her eyebrows and glanced down at the dress she was wearing, the color of the morning glory. "I'm delighted to tell you, Sonia. I bought it when I was on holiday at Curt's. It's not haute couture like Midge's Donna Karan, but even so it broke my budget."

"And worth every penny of it," Curt said smoothly.

"Amazing!" Sonia drawled. "You never used to bother."

Rachael walked to the sofa, convinced Sonia would go to her grave still making catty remarks. "So far I've never had the time. Now I'm going to buy something attractive whenever I can afford it."

"You look marvelous dressed up," Midge said, joining Rachael. "You could be a model."

"Modelling has no value," Sonia pronounced in her dogmatic way, taking little account of Midge's feelings.

"I wouldn't say that," Midge responded with a show of spirit.

"What's it to be, ladies?" Curt broke in, getting to his feet. "Sonia has made up a pitcher of dry martinis."

"Mineral water will do for me," Rachael said, taking the opportunity to squeeze Midge's hand. "One martini, and nothing I say makes sense."

"A glass of white wine for me." Midge looked up at Curt before transferring her attention to the charming, spacious room. "This is a beautiful room, Sonia. Did you do the decorating yourself?"

Poor old Midge! She's put her foot in it again, Rachael thought.

Sonia didn't answer for what seemed a long time. Then she gave Midge a tight smile. "It was Rachael's mother who did that. Some things aren't quite right, but my husband would never have them changed."

"I think it's perfect," Midge answered with what must have been a little intentional malice of her own.

The silence would have grown heavy, only Scott chose that moment to bound into the room. "Sorry I'm late!"

"That's all right, darling," Sonia said fondly. "How I love the holidays when you're home."

Ten minutes later, they were all seated at the gleaming dining room table with the paintings looking down at them from all four walls.

"Isn't this superb!" Midge exclaimed. "At home I have tea in the kitchen. Mum and Dad both work, so they often meet up and eat out."

"And what does your father *do*?" Sonia asked in a voice so condescending Rachael gritted her teeth. She sensed Curt's eyes on her, but avoided his gaze. Could he really find Sonia's snobbishness attractive?

"Midge's father is in real estate," Scott hastened to the defense of Midge's parents. "Her mother has her own hair-dressing salon."

"How interesting!" Sonia said, obviously not interested at all.

"She'd go mad about your hair, Rae," Midge said, clearly deciding to ignore Sonia's brand of snobbery. "You've got the best head of hair I've ever seen. And the color! It's like red wine held up to the light."

Sonia changed the subject soon after that, and the meal progressed quite pleasantly through the tomato-and-basil soup, the fillet of beef with a thick pepper crust, green beans in chive butter, mustardy baked potatoes, and julienned carrots and parsnips, nicely glazed. They were enjoying a lime *bavarois* when Rachael swung her head toward the French doors. She held her head at an odd listening angle.

"What's that?" she asked in an electrified voice.

Sonia, who had begun a story and would have to start all over again, looked annoyed. "Why don't you go and check? I heard nothing."

"Listen." Rachael held up her hand.

It had to be catching, for Curt's relaxed expression now mirrored Rachael's. His hands tensed on the arms of the carver chair.

"Is there something I'm missing?" Sonia asked blankly.

"Who cares? Let's eat," Scott said. "I just hope there's a cheese platter and maybe some fresh figs."

Rachael jumped up, blue eyes blazing, face flushed with color. "That's *rain!*"

"Isn't it, by God!" Curt said very quietly, though his whole manner was overlaid by excitement.

"Rain! Can't you smell it?" Without apology Rachael flew away from the table, heading toward the veranda.

Curt followed.

"Well!" Sonia said in a tight voice. "This is what we've all been waiting for, isn't it?" She sounded irritated that the dinner party had been interrupted.

"I swear you'll never make a station wife, Mum!" Scott went to pull back Midge's chair. "I just hope Rae's right. I can't hear a thing."

In the purple darkness, heavy with the sharp odor of ozone, Curt joined Rachael as she leaned against the wrought-iron railing. Nothing was said, but joy and excitement passed between them like a live electric current. The long wait was over!

The odd murmuring the nature-attuned Rachael had felt before she actually heard it became a dull roar, intensifying in strength until the very air and earth vibrated. The temperature abruptly dropped. None of them stirred; only Scott reached back to switch on the exterior lights that flooded the main compound.

Suddenly they saw it—a great curtain of silver rain, amazing in its density as it advanced from the northeast like an army on the march.

Shivering, Midge fell back against Scott's shoulder, muttering over and over again, "It's unbelievable!" From the balustrade Rachael cried jubilantly, *"Rain!"* She turned to Curt, who in full view of the others, pulled back her long hair and kissed her on the mouth.

Barely noticed by anybody, Sonia withdrew to the dining room, looking as though a sliver of ice had pierced her heart.

Someone in the stockmen's dormitory began banging a drum, the primal voice of the didgeridoo taking up the muffled sounds of the thunder. On a great wave of emotion, Rachael broke Curt's strong grasp, flinging off her shoes and racing down into the tumult, where she began leaping and dancing like an exultant young *lubra* at a successful rain ritual.

"Come, Namarrkon. Come, Jambuwal, the thunder man. Come, Boogoodoo, and Gandah, the rainbird. Make a flood for our rivers, our creeks!"

Midge burst out laughing, but she was close to tears. As a spectacle it was riveting. Rachael, dancing, splashing, shimmering in a spotlight, raising her slender arms to the teeming heavens, bowing to the soaked earth, scooping up silver puddles and letting them cascade down over her streaming head. She looked totally uninhibited, unconscious of her audience, her body moving like a Balinese dancer's. One hand came up to push the weight of her sodden mane to one side. Her face looked ecstatic, her arms and slender hips moving to age-old rhythms inside her head.

"Come in, you little pagan!" Scott called, unable to keep the laughter out of his voice. "Say, where's Mum?" he asked Midge, who was still staring transfixed at Rachael.

"I think she went back into the house."

The noise at the men's compound was growing to a deafening roar. Saucepans had joined the drums. Nat, the jackeroo, was playing his trumpet, a reveille of some kind. Someone started to sing "Waltzing Matilda" in a rousing baritone, and the other men took it up, not roughly, but like a trained choir. It was so stirring, so moving, the tears ran down Rachael's face to merge with the rain.

Miriwin went wild—a state of affairs that was repeated all over the outback as the rain continued to thunder down on a savagely parched land. Eventually the tempest grew so violent and Midge's shivers tore so hard at her body she and Scott were forced to retreat to the house, expecting Rachael and Curt to follow. But Curt, already wet from his lashing at the balcony, went down the steps at a leap, gathering Rachael into his body and pulling her under the wide awning.

"That dance was unforgettable!" he cried exultantly. "I'll remember it every time I close my eyes."

Even soaked as they were, the heat of him enveloped her so all she could do was bask in it. She threw up her head, in a frenzy of desire, inviting him to kiss her, which he did until she crumpled against him, aroused to an exquisite pitch. She could feel the hard muscles straining tautly beneath his skin. Her own clothes were so fused to her that when his hands moved compulsively to cup her breasts she cried out breathlessly. She felt giddy with abandonment, glorying in his lovemaking, the power of his touch.

She didn't understand herself why she put up a brief, fierce struggle. His low laughter came as a breath in her ear. "You're a wild one, aren't you? You like danger."

Like it? She craved it. She looked up, her mouth framed for words, only he lowered his head and kissed her again.

The surge of rapture returned. An electric transmission that sent the life force charging through her body. She felt a great urgency to press herself against him, to feel the heat and shape of his hard, thrilling body. There wasn't anything tender or gentle about it. It was as furious and elemental as the silver storm streaming all around them.

They might have continued forever, only some sense of time and place finally triumphed. Curt put her away from him with a kind of ragged determination, so for the first time she had to consider her *own* power. It transformed her. She locked her hands behind his neck, but he brought them down, fervor in his voice.

"One day, Rachael, I'll meet your every need. But for now, the others are waiting for us inside."

"So you turn it on and off at will?"

The brilliant lights from the veranda gilded his coal-black head and glistened the planes and angles of his face. "No, that's the gentleman in me talking."

"I thought we lost him."

It didn't occur to her that he'd lift her, but that was what he did, scooping her up like a wayward twelve-year-old and rushing up the stairs to the comparative protection of the rain-swept veranda.

Rachael clung to him with one arm, laughing. "I just hope there weren't any witnesses to that." Belatedly she stared through the French doors to the softly lit dining room beyond.

"Who were you thinking of, exactly?" Curt asked, his voice ironic. "You make it sound like we were indulging in a secret vice."

"Some people might think we *were!*" she burst out.

"So defensive! We're free agents, Rachael. Now, listen—we'll have to get you dry. You can get a chill when the temperature drops so quickly."

"No, not me. I have enormous resistance." Rachael smiled up at him, a lovely, warm, joyful smile. "Just think of it, Curt. When we wake up in the morning, every creek, every channel, every billabong will be running a bumper. Who wouldn't go mad on a night like this?"

"Well, that's your excuse, then, if we had an audience," he told her.

And as it turned out, they had. When Rachael emerged from a hot bath, she found Sonia waiting for her in the bedroom. Sonia was wrapped in a gorgeous violet satin-and-lace nightgown and matching robe, but her pallor was so pronounced the color made her look sickly.

Rachael positively jumped. "Sonia! You gave me a fright. What's wrong?"

"You don't think I'm here on a *business* matter?" Sonia snapped. Her eyes were moving all over Rachael with an extraordinary mixture of anger and unwilling admiration. Rachael was draped in a pink towel, face and body glowing, her freshly blow-dried hair a tumble of waves and curls. Sonia clenched her hands. "What the devil do you think you're up to?" she demanded.

"Up to? What?" Rachael retreated to the dressing table, feeling at a distinct disadvantage dressed in a towel that didn't even clear her knees.

"I'll thank you not to play games," Sonia said wrathfully. "There is no way, *no way in this world,* I'm going to stand by and watch you throw yourself at Curt Carradine."

Rachael swung about, her own temper rising. "You're suggesting I am? Isn't that a bit like the pot calling the kettle black?"

"I beg your pardon!" Sonia said in a clipped, outraged voice. "No one could accuse *me* of wild behavior. I've never literally thrown myself at a man in my life. Much less hung around his neck."

"So you were spying?" Rachael said flatly. "Isn't there something a little sick about that?"

Sonia pulled her robe angrily about her. "How dare you make such a fool of yourself? Of this house?"

"Well, if you want to know, it was easy."

Sonia sprang up and turned her face away. "I won't have this kind of disgusting behavior! I'm furious with you, Rachael. Can't you see that?"

"I can see it, Sonia. I don't understand it. You have no right to be furious with me. All the time I was growing up, you wouldn't have this and you wouldn't have that. Where I was concerned, you put your foot down pretty hard. But your reign's over."

"Is it?" Sonia whirled about. "Aren't you forgetting I'm Scott's mother? I have ten times more influence with him than you have. I could make a lot of trouble for you, Rachael."

"You mean behind the porcelain facade lurks the wicked stepmother?"

"Go on, have your little joke. You've always been quick with the flip responses."

"It's a pity *you* don't have a better sense of humor." Rachael turned her back and shouldered into her green kimono, letting the damp towel drop to the carpet.

"Don't think I've forgotten your schoolgirl crush on Curt any more than he has. He's only using you. You'll finish up a laughingstock."

"You mean I'll join the legions who've already made fools of themselves?" She gave Sonia a pointed glance, then sighed and said more quietly, "You don't have to worry, Sonia. I've done nothing to be ashamed of."

Sonia's wild crack of laughter was startling to hear. "You let him *devour* you. Touch your breasts. What else has he done to you?"

"You ought to go straight into therapy, Sonia," Rachael suggested. "It's none of your business. Or, if you're so interested, why don't you go and ask Curt? Not likely! He might prove too tough. Much better to storm in here letting off steam. Do you know what, Sonia? You're jealous."

"Me, jealous?" Sonia sounded frantic.

"Yes, jealous." Rachael felt a rush of pity. "I'm sorry, Sonia. I really am. I'm trying to understand—"

"*You* understand?" Sonia's pale blue eyes widened in scornful disbelief. "What insight could you possibly have into me?"

"Let's stop now, Sonia. We'll only be sorry in the morning."

But Sonia's blood was up. "There's been a big change in you since you came back from his beach house. You slept with him, didn't you?"

"Of course I did!" Rachael took a brush to her hair, turning so she could look at herself in the mirror.

Behind her Sonia dropped like a stone into an armchair. "Is that the truth?" She sounded more desperate than shocked.

"No, it isn't." Rachael didn't have the heart or mind to persist with a lie. "One of the reasons was that he didn't ask me. You know what a gentleman Curt is."

"He didn't look like a gentleman tonight," Sonia replied with dreadful intensity. "I wanted to fly downstairs and pull you apart. Of course, I know what he sees in you. Young face. Young body. That's something I can't compete with. Not anymore. Ten years ago, it would have been quite a different tale. It's hell, hell, I tell you, to watch yourself aging. The slackness, the extra wrinkle. A woman reaches forty and no one thinks of her as a sexual creature. It's like peering down a black stairwell."

"Sonia, you look marvelous!" Rachael tried to console her.

"You mean, for my *age*."

"We all age, Sonia, no matter how much we want to resist it. You're too hard on yourself."

Sonia shrugged, obviously unwilling to let her quarrel go. "Jumping up from the table like that," she fumed. "Dancing in the rain. That was meant to be arousing."

Rachael's face brightened with wry humor. "Listen, my teeth were chattering all the time. It was fun, Sonia. The whole station went wild, in case you didn't hear. You've never understood what rain means. Rain is our lifeblood. It means prosperity for the outback. For Miriwin. It means feed for lots of animals that might otherwise have died. You've never watched their suffering, have you? You don't even venture outside the main compound anymore."

"Don't try to change the subject," Sonia snarled, giving Rachael a wild stare. "I don't give a damn about the cattle. That's no secret."

"Listen, don't tell me, tell Curt. If you're looking for a way to endear yourself to him, tell you don't give a damn about the suffering cattle. He'll *love* that. It's a mystery to me, given the way you feel that you've set your sights on Curt at all."

"Then let me spell it out for you. He *excites* me. My heart races every time I see him. Life with Curt would never be dull like it was with your father."

"No, and it wouldn't work out, either," Rachael said hotly. "You didn't give Dad much peace."

"A false assumption, Rachael. *Your mother* didn't give your father much peace. There are lots of things, my dear, that you don't know. When I was your age, I thought I was entitled to live happily ever after—but I didn't know about the passion Alec still felt for a dead woman. She didn't exist, yet she moved around this house as though she still lived here. She refurbished the place soon after they were married. Your father never would have it changed. I got my way in most things, but never that. Then as you got older, I started to see your mother through your father's eyes. You're beautiful in your way. I've seen the men staring at you, even with your hair in a rubber band. It's a very strange feeling living with your predecessor's double."

The room was humming with old emotions and new tensions, thanks to a complex past that was only now beginning to unravel. "I'm sorry, Sonia. I never knew about any of this."

"Is it any wonder I want to embark on a different life? It's not the past I want to talk about tonight. It's the present. My future. I know Curt's not in love with me now, but he could be. I'm an experienced woman, and I realize that. That's why I don't want you getting in the way with your youth and your raw sexuality. You're just a distraction. Nothing more. As for that girl, Midge—ridiculous name when you're six feet tall—I'll find some way of getting rid of her. How Scotty became involved with her I can't imagine. She's simply not suitable."

With that, she got up abruptly and slammed out of the room.

Rachael was alone for all of five minutes before Scott appeared at her door.

"I just saw Mum flying down the hallway like a bat out of hell. What's up?"

Rachael stood back so he could come in. "There's a lot of anger and resentment locked up inside her."

"You look pretty upset." Scott studied his stepsister closely. "I just knew Mum was spoiling for a fight. Is there ever going to be any peace in this house? No wonder I don't want to come home."

"Well, I consider myself easygoing." Rachael padded back to the bed and sat on it. "Sonia's been the catalyst in our lives."

"Don't I know it!" Scott all but flung himself into a chair. "Mum can be really awful if she doesn't get her own way. I'm starting to wonder if I can stick it out till Christmas."

"Scotty, you've got to stay!" Rachael felt sick with dismay.

"With Mum being so bitchy to poor old Midge? She's so good-natured she won't say anything, but I feel for her. That bit about 'What does your father do?' Mum's such a snob. Midge's dad is as sharp as they come, and her parents have a really good marriage."

"Talk to Sonia about it," Rachael suggested. "Say it's causing you grief that she's giving Midge such a hard time."

"She's not exactly friendly to you, either. Is it something to do with Curt?"

"Yeah," Rachael said dryly.

"I suppose because he kissed you?"

Rachael nodded. "Sonia has her own little fantasy about Curt."

"And that's all it is, Rae!" Scott protested. "Fantasy. At the moment Mum's like an out of control car, but she'll right herself eventually. I'm prepared for her to remarry, but not Curt. Mum's only courting trouble. Oh, I hate this!"

Scott moaned. "Here we are, all rummaging around a huge house, and not one of us doing as we like."

"Scotty, it's time for you to make decisions that are going to affect all of us. Is this trip to New York still on?"

Scott locked his hands behind his head and stared at the ceiling. "Oh, I don't know. It seemed like a good idea before I came home, but I can feel Dad and his disapproval all around me."

"He left you Miriwin. You have to take up your responsibilities."

Scott's attractive face twisted in a grimace. "You should have been the son, Rae. Your heart's in it. Mine isn't. The land isn't in my blood. You're the real Munro. I take after Mum."

"Then you should have had the guts, Scotty, to tell Dad how you felt."

"And risk putting Mum in a rage, let alone the old man? If we're talking guts, I guess you got that, as well. Frankly, Dad scared me stiff. Some days it was a real struggle not to shake. Being around Dad was like being in the army. What a fate!" He sighed. "Maybe the best thing we could do is sell out. Mum tells me Curt might be interested."

Rachael threw up her head, her voice becoming very crisp. "I think Sonia's trying to manipulate us all. I've asked Curt whether he's planning to make an offer, and he denies it."

"Well, wouldn't he—until he's ready to show his hand. The Carradines have always had an eye on Miriwin."

"Surely denying it is unprincipled, isn't it?" Rachael argued. "Does that sound right to you? Curt Carradine lying?"

"Well . . . no," Scott answered, "but maybe he and Mum are trying to negotiate a contract."

"Without telling you? Without telling either of us?"

Scott looked confused. "She knows my feelings about taking over from Dad, Rae. She is my mother, after all, and she has my best interests at heart. No one can doubt that."

"So what are you really saying, Scotty?" Rachael demanded.

Scott thought long and hard. "I'm saying, Rae, I don't think I'm made of the right stuff, but if it means so much to you, I'm prepared to give it a go."

"Before or after New York?"

Scott folded his well-shaped hands. "You could hang on for a while longer, couldn't you?"

"Scotty, when the accountants' report comes in, we might be in for a few shocks."

"Who says?" Scott's dismay was evident.

"Curt dropped a few hints. Dad did confide in him."

"Hell!" Scott leaned forward, staring at his sister. "I knew Dad had his setbacks, but I didn't think anything was seriously wrong."

"Probably it isn't, but the place *has* run down. We need an injection of capital and a lot of hard work. A new manager to replace Matt while he's off—someone who can pick up immediately where Matt left off. We need direction—"

"And you want it from *me*?" Scott rolled his eyes heavenward. "Rae, I don't mind playing Munro of Miriwin, in fact I quite enjoy it, but I'm no great shakes at slaving my guts out. That's no life at all."

"In the end you might find yourself."

Scott looked ruefully at his sister. "You can't put into me what isn't there, Rae. Dad made that mistake."

"He chose to trust you with Miriwin. The Munros have been here a long time. Keeping the Carradines out."

"I thought you were in love with the guy," Scott said calmly.

"I couldn't love someone who was threatening me. Plotting behind my back."

Scott searched her serious face. "Then I hope for your sake that Mum's been telling the odd lie."

CHAPTER SIX

THE NEWS FOR MATT wasn't good. He was referred to a specialist in Brisbane. The very next day Rachael organized a charter flight to the state capital, and a worried Matt and Wyn were on it.

While anxiety swept Rachael, Sonia's reaction was pretty well in character. "How are we supposed to manage?" She treated Rachael to a this-is-your-fault sort of state. "And just how much is that charter flight going to cost? You're so high-handed, Rachael. Now that your father's gone, you seem to think you can make all the decisions. You didn't discuss this with me at all."

"The operation is urgent, Sonia," Rachael explained patiently. "Matt couldn't sit around waiting for a casual lift. I mentioned it at least four times. You could have been more caring, too. Matt and Wyn have been slaving for us for nearly twenty years."

"They've been well paid, haven't they? It wasn't slave labor, as far as I know. Besides, you were making such a fuss I didn't think either of them needed any kind words from me. I only make them nervous. I have that effect on ordinary people."

"Maybe 'nervous' isn't quite the right word," Rachael suggested dryly.

"'Overwhelmed,' then." Sonia carried a pile of magazines to a sofa and sat down. "You can pay for that charter flight, Rachael. The station won't."

"The station will. Scotty agrees. And for now, I'll take over Wyn's role. Or as much as I can manage. There are only four of us. We can take turns to cook."

Sonia slapped the pages of *Tatler* together. "Do you *mind?*" Her face went slack with disbelief. "I have no intention of working the kitchen. I only go there to give orders. Talk to dear Midge. She'd look lovely in a big apron. There's the baking, too. The washing and ironing. The kitchen gardens. Who's going to handle all that?"

"I admit, it's a challenge! All right, so you're not involved. Doesn't it bother you to be so... helpless?"

Sonia smiled sweetly. "Not at all. I know things, Rachael, that you'll never learn."

"That's all right, Sonia. I won't hold it against you. Have a good time." Rachael swung into the hallway and disappeared down the front steps.

THE RAINS CONTINUED, and Rachael spent a good deal of time on horseback, checking on the cows and their calves. Formerly yellow stubble, the plains were now covered in lush Mitchell grass, and the mare cut through a great crush of rain-wet wildflowers, releasing their wonderful, aromatic fragrance. For almost every mile she rode, flocks of budgerigar were her companions, brilliant flashes of green and gold against a pearl-gray sky. Although the rain was still falling all over the outback, it had lost a good deal of its intensity and moving around was much easier. Every river and waterway ran deep with swirling water. It was a glorious sight.

As she rode, Rachael went over all that was happening in her world. This was a turning point in all their lives. She found herself soaking up the beauty and brilliance of her beloved Miriwin as if she would never see it again. It could well be lost to her. She had to face it. Her father had not only betrayed her, he had betrayed their heritage. He might just as well have sold up.

Rachael tied the mare to a tree just outside the high wrought-iron fence that guarded the Munro family cemetery. Among the graves, were little ones, three of them, watched over by white marble angels. Her mother, so sweet and mysterious a figure, was not there. Her distraught parents had claimed her, perhaps ranting at her husband for causing her death. Rachael knelt at her father's tomb. Alexander Clive Munro. Strange beloved man. He'd suffered a terrible loss and carried the marks of it to his grave. She had brought armloads of wildflowers, and now she scattered them over her dear dead. Eyes, nose and throat were scalded by tears. And she was expected to *leave* them! Sixteen of her family! It was like being flayed raw.

Rachael climbed back into the saddle and continued on her way. Even with her oilskin she was feeling faintly chilled, evidence of her state of mind and the water-laden atmosphere. She glanced quickly at her watch. It was later than she thought—time to be getting back. She wondered what Scott and Midge were going to concoct for dinner. One thing was certain, they would enjoy themselves while they were doing it. She smiled at the thought, then frowned. Scott still hadn't told Sonia of his plans. He avoided confrontations like the plague. He'd leave it to the last minute, probably as he was walking out the door. Rachael knew in her heart that he wouldn't stay. Hadn't it always been apparent how badly he wanted a *different* life?

Rachael was skirting Marbuck Creek when she saw a cow and its half-hidden calf lying in a thick tangle of bent grasses and white candytuft. She made her way toward them, and neither cow nor calf made any attempt to bound away. Rachael slipped down from the saddle, realizing as she approached that the cow was dead and the calf badly distressed. Yet there was no real fear in its enormous eyes. It looked exactly as though it had been waiting for her to turn up and rescue it.

"You're all right, little one. I'm here to get you." She moved toward the baby animal, speaking soothingly, when the mare suddenly whinnied sharply, perhaps smelling death. The calf tottered to its feet and began to slip-slide down the wet grassy slope. Then to Rachael's dismay it plunged with a sickening splash into the torrent, lowing pathetically.

"Damn!" Rachael ran after the calf without hesitation. She lost her own balance on the slippery grade, sliding toward the fast-running creek. It flashed through her mind that the water was carrying a lot of debris, but she managed to anchor herself, throwing off hat, boots and oilskin. Then she slid down the rest of the bank into the water. It was so cold she cried out, but she was a strong swimmer and she knew every turn of the creek like the back of her hand.

She struck out, moving swiftly toward the calf that was now mute with terror. "Hang on, little one. I'm coming!" She repeated it in her head, not seeing the all-but-submerged, forked brown limb that suddenly reared up in the air as she and the calf slammed into it. The calf was caught and held, but Rachael hit her head so hard she heard the crack a second before her immediate world went dark.

WHEN CURT ARRIVED at Miriwin with a new mechanic he had recommended for the station, he learned that Sonia was lying down in a darkened room with one of her migraines and Rachael was out "rounding up cows."

Scott and Midge were in the kitchen, Scott fooling around with a food processor, Midge making trial runs with some dough and a pastry wheel.

"We're making ravioli for dinner. Tryin' to, anyway." Midge smiled. "It's about time Rae had a break. She's been doing all the cooking—and darn good she is, too."

"I think I'll go and find her," Curt said. "The rain's coming down harder with nightfall. A flash flood could trap her. Did she say where she was going?"

"Nope. Just checking on the cows and calves," Scott offered. "Don't worry about, Rae, Curt. She's an expert."

"Do you mind if I take the Jeep?" Curt asked in a rather clipped voice.

"Go right ahead." Scott smiled nervously. "Rae knows every inch of Miriwin."

"That's okay when it's not flooded." Curt's face looked unaccountably grim.

Afterward he could never say why he headed toward Marbuck Creek when Rachael could easily have returned across the valley. From the top of the ridge he scoured the empty plains, looking for a familiar slender figure on a chestnut mare. The rain had become heavier, and the churning channels were formidable. There was, despite the heat of the day, an oddly chill wind. Curt stood outside the Jeep, bareheaded, but wearing an oilskin. A violent spatter of rain drenched the field glasses he had trained on the valley. Although he liked Scott and had known him all his life, he had experienced difficulty not showing his reaction to the boy's careless attitude toward his sister. Now, with the rain, dusk was closing in fast. And Rachael would be exhausted if she'd spent the day chasing up cattle.

Never a man to panic, he had to admit to a certain anxiety; pressure lines had formed around his nose and mouth. Even the radiance of great tracts of wildflowers made more luminous by the gray world diminished in the face of his mounting alarm. He felt somehow directed toward Marbuck Creek. The Jeep plunged and bucked across the valley floor, cutting a great swath through the glory of the flowers. As he neared the swollen stream, rising fast now, he stopped the Jeep and began to call out, the old bushman's call, holding his hands to his mouth.

"Coo... eee... coo... eee... coo... eee!"

Nothing. No response from anywhere. The muscles along his taut jawline worked. Where was she? He was positive somewhere near. So positive he didn't stop to wonder about it.

He came on the dead cow first, then as he drove parallel to the stream, he caught sight of Rachael's head and arm. She was wedged into the fork of a half-submerged branch. Her eyes were closed and a runnel of blood was seeping from a wound in her head.

He slid deep into the turgid water, amazed the force of the current hadn't dislodge the branch. He found as he neared her, with some difficulty despite being a powerful swimmer, that the thick end of the branch was braced against one of the large boulders that dotted the white sand. That had saved her.

The swollen creek was racing with debris. He would be no use to her if he cracked his head or limbs. Wind and water whipped his face, yet he reached her. He eased her out of the forked limb, his arm locked around her in a lifesaving hold. The banks of the creek were badly overhung, the soil eaten away by the action of the rushing stream. Valiantly he steered them toward the most accessible slope. Rachael appeared to be unconscious, or slipping in and out of it. She was very cold. God only knew how much water she'd swallowed. His body responded with a man's primitive strength and savagery in the face of the elements.

He clambered out almost breathless, lifting her higher in his arms and carrying her to the sheltered side of the Jeep. He laid her on her back, ran his finger into her mouth to clear it of any obstruction, before beginning artificial respiration. The kiss of life. Her normally golden skin was waxen, and she looked strangely childlike, her beautiful red hair darkened and spread out around her. Blood was still running onto her temple and cheek.

Swiftly he tilted back her head. He pinched her small nostrils, took a deep breath, then placed his mouth over hers. Time was vital.

An eternity seemed to pass before Rachael started to exhale and vomit water. Then he turned her head and body to one side.

"Fight, Rachael," he said in a low, intense voice. "Come on, *fight*. Do it for me."

When she opened her eyes they seemed purple, not blue. "Curt!" Her voice was a soft rasp, evidence that her throat was very sore from the water that had gotten into her windpipe. "The calf?" She was dazed, but coherent.

"Don't worry about the calf," he told her grimly. "You're almost frozen!" He wrapped his oilskin around her like a shawl. "It's an absolute mystery to me how I found you so easily."

"Didn't you hear me calling your name? I was screaming it. Everything was flickering and dimming. The creek was like the sea!" She started to struggle a little, unaware of what she was doing.

He found himself thinking she could not have endured much more. The branch would have given way and the rushing water would have claimed her. He gripped her tightly and rose to his feet. There were many unknowable things in life. Her silent screams, for they had been silent, had reached him.

AT THE HOMESTEAD, an unusually chastened Scott and Midge sprang into action, Scott to hunt up suitable dry clothes for Curt and Midge to run a steaming hot bath for an extraordinarily fragile-looking Rachael. To date, Midge had only been witness to Rachael's competence and vitality; now she was shocked by the stark contrast. She followed Curt as he carried Rachael right into her bathroom, supporting her in a chair while Midge ran the bath, throwing in some herbal bath salts for good measure.

Rachael glanced up into Curt's set face. One could only describe his handsome features as determined and grim. "You're not going to take my clothes off, are you?" She said it as a joke, but his expression precluded any humor.

"Midge will help you do that. Get in the bath, Rachael, and soak. I'll have to do something about that wound in your head. A few stitches. I've learned all about it. Thank God it's in your hair and not on your face, otherwise I mightn't be game to touch it."

Midge glanced over, wide-eyed. "Isn't it going to hurt?"

"Of course it's going to hurt," Rachael jeered softly. "He doesn't care. No problem, is it, Curt?"

"No, but I'm not going to enjoy it." He straightened up and walked to the door of the adjoining dressing room. "I'll be close by, Midge, if you need any help. She's not as tough as she likes to make out."

"I won't faint," Rachael insisted.

Midge looked at her carefully. "I'm not so sure, but I think I can handle the situation, Curt. I'm pretty strong, you know. I work out."

At this point, Sonia, dressed in a gauzy blue-and-pink caftan, appeared behind Curt's shoulder. Her face was showing the effects of her severe headache. She looked white and pinched, with dark circles beneath her eyes.

"What on earth is going on?" she asked in a strained voice. Her gaze swept all of them, but she addressed Curt.

He answered briskly. "Rachael has had an accident, Sonia. She went into the creek chasing up a calf. She struck her head, and she's suffering from hypothermia and perhaps concussion. She needs a hot bath."

"Rachael has had an accident?" she repeated hysterically. "Why must she put herself in such awful danger? Can anyone answer me that? Who could possibly care about a calf? It's utterly absurd. Rachael's escapades have plagued us for years. I shouldn't have to endure this when I'm far from well."

Curt put a hand to her shoulder. "Go back to your room, Sonia. There's nothing you can do here. You're on medication for the migraine?"

"If it would only work!" Sonia leaned toward him apparently oblivious of his wet clothing. "You're such a comfort to me, Curt."

Midge moved swiftly and shut the bathroom door. "Boy," she said to Rachael, "isn't Sonia some piece of work! She's not the least bit worried about you."

"Tell me something I *don't* know," Rachael croaked.

"Just as well you have Curt to turn to."

"Observe how sweet he was to Sonia." Feeling faint and exhausted, Rachael pulled at her shirt.

"He humors her, that's all. It's not like with you—he was worried sick. Here, sweetie," she murmured, "let me help you. All set? Let's go!"

RACHAEL AWOKE ABRUPTLY around daybreak, feeling sick and disoriented. She sat straight up in bed, holding her bruised throat. She'd come pretty close to dying down there at Marbuck Creek, but she couldn't quite take it in. She remembered the rushing water and the howling wind. The terrible frustration of not being able to keep her eyes open. And a long time after that—Curt. She remembered lying back on the wet grass with the fragrant crush of wildflowers beneath her, staring up into his face. It seemed to her that his strong features were modeled in granite. Only his golden eyes were brilliant and lustrous. She knew he had saved her life. Somehow she had made him hear her cries. It was extraordinary. It filled her with an almost spiritual certainty. Even his presence suffused her bedroom like incense. She remembered the moment he had said good-night to her. Not a trace of lightness or a smile to be seen. He had been very quiet, hiding his inner feelings. The odd thing was, she knew he was suffering. Coming on her like that must have been a shock.

The door to her bedroom was open, but she was quite alone. She knew someone had been sitting in her armchair, because a mohair rug was flung across it and her small bedside lamp was burning on the table, casting a soft glow across the room. She had been under supervision all the hours she had slept so heavily. Rachael put up a hand. She felt cold, but her cheeks were hot. Even her breath was coming in harsh little gasps. It seemed there were going to be consequences to her little escapade, as Sonia had put it. At the very least, a bad cold.

Where were the painkillers? She recalled seeing them on her bedside table last night. They weren't there now. Only a jug of water and a glass. Rachael threw back the covers and slid out of bed, standing shakily on her feet. She felt an ache, like a weight pressing on her skull.

She couldn't be bothered pulling on her robe. Who was around to see her? Obviously, whoever had been watching her from the armchair had felt satisfied that she'd been comfortably asleep. Rachael padded across the carpet, putting her head around the door. Lights were burning at either end of the hallway, which was more a long gallery connecting both wings of the house. An imposing lineup of

Munro portraits stared down from the walls; she barely glanced at them or at the collection of Scottish baronial chairs, and the console bearing two spectacular bronze urns.

She would have to go down to the kitchen. Wyn kept a well-stocked medicine chest on the top shelf of the walk-in pantry. Rachael turned to close her door, but when she straightened her head, expecting an empty, deeply shadowed hallway, she was stunned to see a woman emerging from the guest bedroom that was always reserved for Curt.

For a moment Rachael thought she was going to faint. Despite the chill on her body, she broke out in a sweat. In this instance it was horror and powerful feelings of shock and betrayal. She wanted to scream out a protest, but not even a moan passed her lips. Sonia, blond head lowered, was flying down the corridor without looking right or left, like a fugitive. She was wearing one of her many ravishing nightgowns, and the peignoir was floating behind her like a bridal train. Within seconds she disappeared, finding refuge within the master bedroom at the farthest end of the west wing.

Dear God! Only now did a suffering prayer move Rachael's lips. She fell blindly back into her room, leaning against the tall chest of drawers, putting a hand to her distressed heart. It was thudding so painfully it felt as though she were receiving a series of blows.

Curt and Sonia? She was overcome by a sick, searing anguish. Had Curt responded to Sonia's desire, or had that desire been in him all along? What did she really know about human behavior? For that matter, what did she know about sexuality?

There was an odd taste in her bruised throat. With a groan she turned and made a run for her bathroom where she threw up acrid bile. Now at last, however searing to her ego, she knew where she stood. Curt had used his power over her, but only as leverage. He would never get the chance again!

She staggered back to her bed and fell into a fitful sleep.

By midmorning her condition had deteriorated, so Curt made the decision to fly her to Kiparra Base Hospital.

"Better than risking pneumonia," Midge said worriedly. Generally so vital, Rachael looked sick and withdrawn.

"Sure you don't want us to come with you?" Scott asked.

"No thanks, Scotty. You have a lot to talk to your mother about."

Scott looked his surprise. Rachael never referred to Sonia as "your mother," but she did so now with an expression that bordered on contempt. Rachael knew he found it strange, but she couldn't help her reaction or her distant manner with Curt. Scott probably thought it was the blow to her head.

In the end she was admitted for four days, suffering from an upper-respiratory-tract infection that quickly worked its way into her chest. For the first forty-eight hours there was little response to the prescribed antibiotics, but when the medication was changed, her system began to fight back. There was no serious injury to her head. The doctor complimented Curt on the neatness of his stitching.

The day before Rachael was discharged, Matt underwent his operation. The following day, Curt brought her the news that Matt's surgeon was very pleased with the way things had gone. He expected Matt to make a satisfactory recovery. A course of physiotherapy would follow, but the doctor did not recommend returning to a life of long hard hours in the saddle. The repaired limb would not stand up to that kind of stress.

"We'll find something for him," Rachael said, throwing her things into a carryall. "I could have caught a charter flight back, Curt. There was no need for you to come for me. No need at all."

He glanced at her averted profile. "That doesn't sound very friendly."

"It's pathetic the way we've come to rely on you."

"You're angry with me. Why?"

"I'm not angry at all," Rachael said with cool dignity. "Thank you for bringing me news of Matt. I'll speak to him as soon as I can. I take it you didn't tell him or Wyn about my misadventure."

"I thought they had enough to handle. You can say as much or as little as you like."

She colored at his ironic tone. "Home again. I can't believe all that's happened to me."

"You're lucky to be alive," he said in a clipped voice, taking the bag from her.

"Thanks to your expertise at playing the hero. Is there no other side to you, Curt?"

"I never know from one day to the next how I'm going to find you, Rachael," he said by way of answer.

"Maybe I could say the same about you," Rachael countered, disenchantment rolling over her like a wave.

"No doubt I'll find out what this is all about in due time," Curt said smoothly, plainly determined to ignore her strange mood. "All you need to do now is try to relax." He took the carryall from her with gentle force. "If you're ready, we'll go. I have a Japanese VIP flying in this afternoon."

She looked up at him with aloof eyes. "I told you you didn't have to worry about me, Curt."

His handsome mouth thinned. "The pity of it is, I do!"

MIDGE HAD GONE to a lot of trouble to prepare a welcome-home lunch, but Curt excused himself almost immediately.

For once Sonia had not been on hand to greet him, and Rachael was glad of it. She could not have endured Sonia's warmth and animation in Curt's presence, the way she constantly brushed his arm with her hand. Indeed, she was going to find it very difficult to act naturally with her stepmother. The incredible shift in Sonia and Curt's relationship was impossible to handle. It seemed, in her emotional state, like various forms of betrayal. She couldn't think through these entanglements. For Curt to tell her unashamedly he worried about *her?* Nothing made sense. It was no basis for her future.

"Everything all right between you and Curt?" Scott asked with obvious bafflement. "You seemed very cool to each other."

"We rely too much on Curt." Rachael's fine-boned face showed traces of her inner tension.

"I suppose we do, but heck, Rae, he saved your life."

"I told him I was grateful."

Midge sought to smooth things over. She looked at Rachael with concern. "You're pale, Rachael. You gave us all a fright. Why don't we start lunch?"

"This looks lovely, Midge," Rachael said sincerely. "You have an artistic flair."

Midge flushed with pleasure and Scott kissed her cheek. "Doesn't she, though! It's great to have you home, Rae. Like Curt said, you're not as tough as we like to think. It was pretty foolhardy going in after that calf."

Rachael shook out her napkin and placed it on her lap. "I couldn't let the poor little thing drown. Curt told me one of the men got a rope on it at the crossing. All's well that ends well, I suppose. Is Sonia going to join us?"

"We can only hope!" Scott said nonchalantly. "I expected her to be on hand to meet Curt, but she must have thought he was staying for lunch. I tried to thank him for doing so much for us all, but he wasn't having any. The famous Carradine charm wasn't in evidence today. I guessed it had something to do with you."

"You guessed wrong."

"Okay!" Scott said mildly. "You're really in a bad mood, Rae. But who could blame you? I've been having nightmares myself. Curt was pretty angry with me, and he didn't try to hide it. Someone needed to stay with you that night, but he didn't trust any of us. He looked in on you most of the time."

"What about *my* shift?" Midge asked.

"You did all right." Scott patted her hand. "The big surprise was Mum got rid of her headache. I remember thinking it left her kinda sudden. She was really carrying on to Curt about how reckless you are."

"He had his old room?" Rachael asked, trying hard to sound offhand.

"Yeah." Scott speared another thick slice of ham. "Always the same one. You have to admit he's been a great friend to us over the years. Dad thought the sun shone out of him. Of course, he was hoping you and Curt might make a go of it one day."

"What utter nonsense!" Rachael said sharply. She had been trying to distance herself from Curt for days.

Scott flashed his beautiful white grin. "Shows what *you* know. Dad thought Curt would be perfect for you."

"He told you that?" Rachael asked with heavy humor.

"He didn't have to spell it out."

"Dad made quite a few mistakes."

"Well, we can fix one of them," Scott said, his voice completely serious now. "The moment I can do something about it, I'm upping your stake in Miriwin by ten percent."

Rachael was silent, staring down at her plate.

"You deserve it, Rae," Midge said anxiously. "It's just terrible how you didn't get an equal share with Scotty. That's what I told him. It's not even as though Scotty's willing to become a cattleman."

"Dad couldn't see that, Midge. Have you discussed this with Sonia, Scotty?"

"Discussed what?" Sonia's soft tones wafted to them from the doorway. "Welcome home, Rachael," she said. "I must say you look peaky. All big eyes and jutting bones."

"And doesn't it suit her!" Midge said aggressively. Two patches of color formed on her cheeks.

"Probably that's the big girl in you talking, Midge." Sonia smiled sweetly. "You won't ever be able to give up on your diet, will you?"

"Yes—just like you," Midge retorted to everyone's surprise.

"That's rather a lot of food for only the four of us," Sonia said with a mock rueful expression. "You must have stripped Wyn's vegetable garden, Midge."

Scott looked at Rachael with angry frustration, but she shook her head.

"What were you talking about when I came in?" Sonia asked.

"I'm planning to increase Rachael's equity in Miriwin," Scott said bluntly.

The muscles of Sonia's small face went rigid. "You're *what?*"

"Precisely ten percent," Rachael answered for her brother.

"He can't! Don't be such a fool, Scott. Obviously she's been working on you."

"*She* has been in hospital for the past four days," Scott said tersely.

"Before then. She's just been waiting for you to come home. That hint about contesting the will was a clever idea. Curt did warn me."

Rachael turned her head away, but Scott looked directly at his mother. "All Rachael did was ask me what I planned to do about Miriwin. She's entitled to know."

"And what are you planning to do?" Sonia asked in a high, challenging voice. "This place is too big for you to work. You don't want to do it. You never did want to do it."

"That's not what you told Dad."

"Thank you very much, Scott. I look after your interest, and that's the sort of thanks I get. I am totally against Rachael's getting a larger share."

"Well, it's not up to you, Mum." For the first time Scott showed signs of standing up to his mother. "As Rachael pointed out, she was the firstborn."

"Oh, that *is* a hefty claim!" Sonia's expression was disdainful. "It's cheap sentiment, and it worked. If you're thinking of upping Rachael's share, I insist I get more, too."

Scott's blue eyes widened. "Hell, Mum, haven't you got enough? All that jewelry. The pick of the paintings. They're all yours. Dad was heavily insured. That's yours. You walked away with a lot."

Sonia's color rose. "Aren't you forgetting I am your father's widow?"

"I thought *you* were the one to forget that!" Rachael flashed.

"How dare you!" Sonia stiffened in outrage. She turned slowly toward Rachael, her eyes glittering like ice floes. "I understand what's happening, of course. You're *sick* with jealousy."

"No way!" Rachael shrugged with commendable coolness, considering the way she felt. "You want to involve yourself with Curt Carradine, that's your business."

"Oh, don't be stupid, Rae." Scott frowned. "Mum's not really serious."

"Aren't I?" Sonia smiled in a most peculiar fashion.

It was too much for Midge. She tried to stand up. "I'll go. These are family matters."

"Sit down, Midge," Scott said sharply. "You're important to me. You can hear every word I have to say."

"The devil she can!" Sonia whirled on her son, an imposing figure for all her tiny frame. "There are things about this family I don't want Midge to know."

"Anything to do with *you?*" Rachael asked.

"The fact is, Mum, I've told Midge everything, but there's something I haven't told you. Midge and I are planning to go to New York early next year."

Midge's face showed her dismay. "Did you have to, Scotty? Right now?"

"When's a good time, Midge?" Rachael asked. "Sonia has to know. We have to decide what's happening to Miriwin."

Sonia threw up her beautifully cared-for hands. "Here we go again! God, Rachael, it's nothing but Miriwin, Miriwin, Miriwin. It will be a real pleasure to get this place off my hands."

"Me, I'm heading for New York," Scott announced.

"Why there?" Sonia asked desperately. "You'll be killed and dumped in the street."

"Sure," Scott said. "Come on, Mum. Midge's sister has survived. She's a top model. We sent over portfolios, and she thinks her agency can get us work."

Sonia looked shocked and deeply offended. "Are you mad, Scott?" she asked. "Models. Portfolios. What kind of sleazy life is that?"

"Sleazy! Top models make a fortune!"

"Speak when you're spoken to, Michelle," Sonia warned. "This is between me and my son. I won't see his life destroyed."

"All I want, Mum, is a bit of fun!" Scott groaned. "To see the world. All my life, I've been told what I'm going to do. What I'm going to be. No one asked *me*. Even Rae thinks I should settle for Miriwin because *she* loves it so much. I realize now I've been trying to please everyone."

"And had a thoroughly good time while you were at it," Rachael pointed out. "So, you want to sell now? Lay it on the line."

Brother and sister stared at each other. "Oh, God, Rae, I wish I could do it. Just for you. But it wouldn't work."

"So it's goodbye to everything the Munros have lived and died for?"

"Such melodrama!" Sonia rolled her eyes. "Accept what you can't change, Rachael. You can't deny that Scotty's the one who'll decide."

"The real decider was Dad," Rachael said. "Even if I'd contested the will—and the thought did cross my mind—I doubt I would've been awarded the controlling interest. No matter what, you and Scotty could always outvote me."

"I'm glad to hear you talking sense," Sonia said sharply. "I've been ready to sell for at least ten years. We could have had lots of money and plenty of comfort."

Midge blinked. "Haven't you *now?*"

No one answered her. Sonia stared at her son with anguished eyes. "When I most need you, you're going away?"

"Mum, I have to live my own life!"

"Do you have to live it at the opposite side of the world?" she demanded.

"We don't plan on staying there, Sonia," Midge said kindly. "We'll be coming home."

"I do not want to hear from you, Michelle." Sonia gritted her teeth.

"That's it! That does it!" Scott jumped up. "I won't have you speaking to Midge like that. I was hoping you'd change, Mum, but you never do. One of these days Midge and I might get married. And if we do, it'll work for us. Not like you and Dad."

"Don't expect me to believe that," Sonia said coldly. "I wouldn't even give you twelve months."

Scott shook his head as if to clear it. "No one can ever win with you, Mum. You always have the last word. Well, if Curt wants Miriwin, he can have it. End of the long wrangle. The Carradines always get what they want, anyway."

"I've worked hard enough on the deal," Sonia said, as though she expected a round of applause.

It was the first time she'd made an actual admission, and Rachael threw up her head, her expression tight with disgust. "So you've been pretending all along, haven't you, Sonia? Working hard on your schemes at my expense. Do you ever tell the truth?"

"A lot of the time, I hope," Sonia drawled, casually adjusting one of her earrings. "Think of it this way, dear. You've been so tedious in your attitude, and I promised Curt I wouldn't talk about our...negotiations. Don't think I'm plagued by guilt. I'm not. I live in the real world, Rachael. Beside me, you're incredibly naive."

"Isn't *that* the truth!" Rachael stood up and walked deliberately from the table.

Christmas was coming up. What a cruel joke!

CHAPTER SEVEN

RACHAEL PUT THROUGH a call to Wyn later that evening. Since Telecom Australia had completed the massive Rural and Remote Areas Program a couple of years before, the outback had reaped the enormous benefits of modern services, benefits the rest of the country took for granted, but that opened up a new way of life for people of the vast interior.

Wyn was full of sad and amusing observations and quick, sharp comment. Matt, she told Rachael, was feeling very thwarted stuck in hospital, where he would remain for several more days. Afterward, as an outpatient he was to have an extensive course of physical therapy, but they'd found a nice place close to the hospital.

Scott hovered in the background while Rachael chatted, but when she mouthed, *would he come to the phone?* he declined with a quick crisscross of his hands.

"How are they?" he asked as Rachael hung up.

"Fine." She spoke briskly, disappointed in his responses. "What's on your mind? Something obviously is."

"I don't think I can take much more of this," he muttered.

"Sounds like you're planning to bolt?"

Scott flushed slightly. "Take it easy, Rae. Mum's acting so badly the sooner we get out the better."

"Yes, it is pretty grim," Rachael was forced to agree. "She resents Midge."

"Find me the person she does like, outside of Curt and her smart friends in Sydney."

"Even they don't see eye to eye with her at times." Rachael started to walk through to the drawing room.

Scott hurried after her, putting a hand on her arm. "Listen, Rae, if it's all right with you, Midge and I are thinking of going back to Brisbane for Christmas. Why don't you come with us? We could show you a good time."

"And leave Sonia by herself? Come off it, Scotty."

"Don't think for one moment she needs *you*."

"No, whatever bond we had seems to be broken. Nevertheless I couldn't leave her. You do what you want to do, Scotty."

Sonia, who had a rare talent for creeping up on people, suddenly appeared at the doorway. "So you're running away again, Scotty?"

Scott's good-looking face looked driven and upset. "It's your own fault, Mum. I hate it when you're rude to Midge."

"Rude?" Sonia's expression was ludicrously outraged, and she moved farther into the room. "Is the girl a marshmallow?"

"You treat her like a rhinoceros. She doesn't deserve it. *Her* mother is super to me."

Sonia smiled. "I expect she's delighted her daughter is having an affair with a millionaire."

Scott's face was utterly transformed by anger and disgust. "They don't give a damn that we own Miriwin."

Sonia waved him away impatiently. "Then why is Midge walking around bug-eyed? For once in your life use your brain. I'll bet she was astonished at what Miriwin might fetch."

Scott flushed. "It's perfectly normal."

"A bad mistake to have told her." Sonia shook her head. "You'll never get rid of her now."

Scott sighed. "It's not Midge I'm worried about. It's *you*, Mum. I knew in my heart coming home was a mistake."

For the first time Sonia looked badly shaken. "Home, where you get so much love and attention?"

"Maybe, but it's claustrophobic."

"How cruel you are, Scotty." Sonia crumpled into a chair. "Sit down, please. We must talk."

Scott hesitated, but Rachael waved him down.

Sonia gave her a grateful smile. "Thank you, Rachael. I didn't think you'd be on my side."

"Christmas won't be Christmas without Scotty. But I don't like your being rude to Midge, either."

"Then I'll apologize!" Sonia exclaimed as artlessly as a child.

Scott gave her a sharp look. "You'd only start again."

"Forgive me, darling. I don't know what gets into me at times." She sat forward, a charming figure in her coral dress. "But you don't make allowances for me, do you? Either of you. You don't consider that this might be a terrible time of my life. Widows have no standing."

"*You* sure do," Scott said, exasperated.

"I was under the impression that you were hotly desired," Rachael added pointedly.

"I may be nearly forty, children, but I'm not dead. All right. As far as Midge is concerned, we'll start over. As for Christmas—I have an idea Curt is going to invite us."

"Leave me out!" Rachael said.

"By all means, if it makes you happier."

"Rae doesn't go, Midge and I don't go," Scott maintained stoutly.

"Don't make it sound like a sacrifice, Scotty."

"Well, you have to admit Curt puts on great parties. It's an honor to be invited."

"Then you must go," Rachael said.

"And you'll reconsider?"

Rachael's eyes were shadowed and distant. "No."

"Then that makes the whole thing null and void. We couldn't leave you on your own."

"We probably could," Sonia said. "Rachael would be perfectly safe. We could even get someone in."

"I shall be perfectly all right on my own."

Sonia turned to her son with a gesture of near despair. "*Please* stay for the holidays, my darling. I promise I'll behave."

And so she did. For a while.

MAINTENANCE ON A STATION is endless. The fencing along the Pingarra Camp was down to three wires. Instead of walking along the fence, the cattle simply stepped through. Rachael detailed two of the men, Jimbo and Charlie, to put down a section to be replaced with a good strong fence the cattle would respect. She rode to the Pingarra Camp mid-morning to check on progress and found the work going well. Around noon when she was thinking of finding a quiet spot to eat her sandwiches, a rider approached them through the curtain of tall trees. All of them looked up, expecting Paddy, who was standing in for Matt, but Paddy didn't look anything like that, nor did he sit so straight in the saddle.

Jimbo lifted an arm. "Hi, there, Mr. Carradine!"

"Jimbo." Curt responded. He dismounted a short distance away, tethering his horse beside Rachael's chestnut mare.

Both stockmen grinned a welcome, showing perfect white teeth, but Rachael's slender body went tense. "How did you find me?" she asked, not realizing her eyes were full of a kind of dismay.

"You mean you were hiding?" His tone was dangerously casual.

Rachael looked back at the stockmen, who were unashamedly listening. "Jimbo, since you're so fond of being boss, you're in charge. Knock off for lunch in about half an hour. I'll be back later this afternoon."

"Sure, Rachael. Don't worry about nothin'," Jimbo doffed his hat. "I'll keep a sharp eye on Charlie here."

"Oh, yeah?" Charlie seemed unimpressed.

Curt and Rachael moved off toward the horses, Rachael intent on retying the bandanna around her neck. "Come to Miriwin for a meeting, Curt?"

"I prefer to call it a visit."

"Give me a break!" She threw up her head, staring into his eyes.

"Rachael," he said, "you sorely try me. I have no idea what you're getting at. I've come to ask you all to be my guests Christmas Day. I thought it would be a sad time for you here—the first Christmas without your father."

"How very kind of you!" Rachael said with magnificent scorn. She turned away abruptly and mounted the mare.

Curt went to the mare's head, holding it. "You seem to have lost your manners."

"I'm planning on having no manners at all." She jerked the reins, turning the mare toward the narrow path.

"So it seems!" Curt called out. A few moments more and he was riding up alongside. "Scott told me I might have to persuade you. Why don't you want to join us?"

"I've become very reclusive."

"I won't argue with that." There was an answering hostility in his voice. "It might help if I told you I'll have house guests. My sisters are coming with their husbands and children. You've always got on well with them."

"A family get-together?"

"As usual."

"I do like your sisters—but believe me, I'd be happier at home."

"You're happy, then?" he asked with harsh incredulity. "You've got shadows under your eyes."

"I'm not sleeping as well as I used to."

"You look as though someone has hurt you very badly." Rachael gave a brief nod. "Don't worry, Curt. I'll survive."

His golden glance burned her. "Survive what, exactly?"

For an instant her expression suggested he was torturing her. "I'm sorry I spoke at all. I'll be honest with you. *Honest!* I appreciate honesty. Scott was thinking of going back to Brisbane. This visit, things haven't been working out that well—until Sonia mentioned your plans for Christmas dinner. Obviously you'd discussed it."

"Wrong!" he said crisply. "Sonia must have guessed I'd do this."

"Why not? You're a very *close* friend."

"Exactly. To you *all.*"

"Not to me," Rachael said in a bleak voice. "Anyway, Sonia loves Scott in her fashion. She wants him with her for Christmas. Scott said he wouldn't go anywhere without me. So on that basis I accept your invitation."

"How bloody insulting!" Curt said with conviction.

"It's the best I can do." She was trembling now and ready to gallop off.

"What's on your mind, Rachael? You think you can solve it by galloping away?"

"I'm tired and I'm hungry."

"Then we'll ride back to the house."

"Not if I can help it!" Rachael flashed. "I'm staying out here where it's safe."

"Did you bring some food with you?" he asked tersely.

"Sandwiches. A drink."

"I hope enough for two." He stared ahead. "You need a chance to catch your breath and talk. It's too damned hot riding this time of day. What about the gully up ahead? We can stop there—it's quiet and peaceful."

There didn't seem to be any way out of it; he was determined to join her. They tethered the horses in the shade of the fragrant limewoods, then moved down to the green oasis of the gully. The surface of the water was sequined with a multitude of colored lights, reflecting the explosion of blossoms on the trees. The sound of the birds enhanced the peace and the breeze carried the delicious aroma of wild fruit.

Rachael's deepest regret was that whatever had been between herself and Curt was now utterly destroyed. Curt Carradine was unattainable. And he always had been. She was discovering something else, too. She didn't want him. She was looking for a different kind of man. A man she could trust and respect.

With natural grace Curt threw down a rug and Rachael began spreading out the contents of her saddlebag—a packet of sandwiches, a thermos of coffee, an apple and a mandarin.

"Okay, that's it. Not exactly a feast." She took off her hat and tossed it behind her. Her hair was back to its easy-care braid, but curly tendrils sprang all around her hairline.

Curt drew the thermos toward him. He poured a cup of coffee into the stainless-steel lid. "Here, drink this."

"You have it." She shrugged, then added. "There's plenty."

"I'll wait until you've finished." He opened the packet of sandwiches, pushing them toward her. "I'm sure you've lost weight again. Have you?"

"Maybe. Because we're eating my cooking, not Wyn's. Have a sandwich, Curt. I won't eat them all."

"Maybe in a second." He, too, swept off his wide-brimmed akubra, laying it on the sand behind him. He stretched out, turning on his side to look at her. Was there ever such a man so stunningly, aggressively *male?*

"Do you mind not staring at me?" Rachael begged. Despite her best efforts, she was filled with a sick longing.

"Sometimes when I look at you I can read what you're thinking."

"You wouldn't like what I'm thinking now."

"You're right!" He turned with one sinuous movement and lay back, his rangy body barely two feet from hers. She could feel his presence like a living force—the tremendous energy that resided in him. Even easier to pick up was the sensuality that could run molten. One of the most difficult things in this life had to be loving a man you also despised. That was the burden she carried. Desire and disgust at either end of the scale. The old hero-worship had become a complex, contradictory emotion, a mixture of love and hate.

She managed another sandwich. Drank the rest of the coffee. It was impossible to relax. Finally she put the mug down and wrapped her arms around her as some form of protection.

"You *are* in a mess, aren't you?"

"I'd be perfectly all right if you'd leave me alone. Here, have your coffee now."

"Why so frantic?"

"Why not? You make it your business to rattle me."

He took the coffee mug, placed his mouth where hers had been. Rachael bit at the shiny red apple. It was crisp, juicy, sweet. The breeze rustled all around them, resembling music. The birds warbled along with it, a small orchestra of piercingly sweet voices. She had to get away from him. From this lovely, cool place. It was vital if she wanted to keep up her illusory detachment.

His hand snaked up, pulled at the thin yellow ribbon that secured her glossy braid. Immediately her hair began to unwind, dark red masses floating down her back.

"When you were a little kid you had more curls than Shirley Temple."

"Who's Shirley Temple?" she joked wryly.

"She was adorable. Full of sparkle. So were you."

"Were? Past tense? That's fine."

"You haven't had a happy life, Rachael," he said quietly.

"I thought I had, but then I didn't know any different. Now I can see how much I've missed."

"Someone's going to make it up to you, Rachael. Do you feel a little better?"

"Actually I feel . . . nervous."

"Surely not on account of me?"

With his eyes on her she couldn't move. This was how a doe felt faced with a lion. The feeling that was pulsing between them was just as primitive. His eyes gleamed against the dark tan of his skin, and the black of his hair and brows was pronounced. He was physically the most arresting man she had ever seen. Even had he been ugly, his voice was enough. Everything about him put terrible pressure on a woman to surrender. Was that what had happened to Sonia? Rachael could understand—but she could never condone it. She likened it to betrayal. Sonia's betrayal to her husband's memory. Curt's to her. She had allowed herself to believe he'd come to care for her, but she'd been disastrously wrong. The caring was no more than common lust. She wanted, needed, a lot more than that. She knew she should get up, get away from him, but his magnetism was so strong it was akin to being held in thrall.

"I don't suppose you'd let me in on your tormented thoughts?"

She shook her head. "Not a one. You're eating all of my apple."

"It's so damned good. Let me peel the mandarin for you."

"I'll do it." She tried desperately to keep her voice casual. "Besides, I'm only following your lead. You're an expert at keeping things to yourself."

"Actions speak louder than words, blue eyes!" he retorted crisply. "Though they're not blue all the time. Sometimes they're like my favorite little gilla flowers. Sometimes they're violet. When you nearly drowned yourself they turned purple in shock. I know women who'd kill for eyes like yours."

"How very foolish." The citrusy smell of the mandarin wafted up from her fingers.

"If you won't tell me your thoughts, I'll have to guess. Is it possible Sonia and Scott are talking about selling?"

His insolence, his *duplicity,* took her breath away. "Don't play the fool with me, Curt. You're the last person in the world it suits."

He didn't raise his voice, but she felt his menace. "Sometimes, Rachael, I could shake you until your teeth rattle. Where do you get off treating me like I'm corrupt? I'll have to put an end to that—though I can see you're upset."

A touch of hysteria crossed Rachael's face. "Well, *you're* no calming influence," she cried aggressively.

"Settle down, Rachael," he warned. "You know what it is, don't you? There's too much emotion between us."

"Emotion?" As she swung her head, her hair fanned out like a cloud. "That's not the way I see it."

"No?" Abruptly he reached for her. He brought her down to him, pressing her back onto the rug while he hung above her, his topaz eyes filled with a brilliant cold light.

"Don't you touch me," Rachael said between clenched teeth. "Here's one woman who isn't shockingly weak."

"The things you say aren't the things you mean."

She stared up at him, her eyes dark with outrage. "You *are* corrupt!" she cried. "A deceiver."

"Hardly. But I'd have to be some kind of a masochist to put up with you."

She could see he was furious, a pallor beneath his polished skin. He wrenched her to her feet and put her forcibly away from him.

She should have been able to retain her balance, but her legs were so wobbly and her emotions in such a tumult she staggered backward. Her riding boot came up against the tip of a half-buried rock with the result that she toppled over it and hit the sand. She went down in a heap, scraping her elbow on the rocky outcrop.

Blood welled, but she felt no pain at all. She burst into the quick emotional tears she so abhorred, shudders running the entire length of her body. She was shamed, sick, confused. Here she was, clasping her moral outrage to her, her righteous feelings, when she was as vulnerable to the agonies of jealousy as any other woman in love. The legs that had been so shaky now felt as if they were made of lead. She couldn't get up. She lay there gulping back tears.

He went to her, picked her up, examined her white, tear-stained face, then her bleeding arm. "What's happening to us, Rachael?" he asked in a quiet voice. "What in God's name is the matter? I'm the same man I've ever been. I have no thought whatever of hurting you."

She stood still while he tied a clean handkerchief around her arm. "I'm sorry," she managed, head bent. "I can't handle this situation at all."

"Maybe you could tell me what 'this situation' is? Why are you crying?"

She dashed her hand across her cheeks. "I have absolutely no idea. Maybe it's all part of being a woman. Go away if you can't live with it." She drew a deep, shuddering breath. "It's been a pretty grim year."

"My God, do you think I don't know that?" he asked in a pent-up voice. "That's enough now, Rachael. You'll make yourself ill. Let alone what it's doing to me."

She sank her teeth into her full lower lip. "I certainly don't want to embarrass you. I know men hate tears."

"They sure do—because they work." With a frustrated exclamation he gathered her into his arms. "You scare me, Rachael."

"Scare the great Curt Carradine?"

"I don't know about that. I'm *me* and I try to be an honorable man."

She stiffened perceptibly and looked up at him, her blue eyes angry and challenging. "So why are you using me? I won't have it. Not anymore."

"Won't you?" Suddenly his temper seemed to flashpoint. He brought down his mouth on hers, punishingly. No tenderness at all. What he offered was a hard male dominance. What he took was the violent pleasure her body was giving him.

Her cotton shirt was hanging loose, inviting the hand that found her swelling breasts. There was so much sensation! Rachael arched convulsively as though shot through with a million volts. He bent her backward over his arm, taking her aroused nipple into his mouth. The sound she made was a primitive little moan. Surges of excitement rushed through her body. His mouth trailed across her electrified skin. Back and forth. She was moving beyond the point where she knew or cared what was going to happen next. Her whole body was curling up. Her limbs turned molten. She was unable to resist him.

Her nails dug into the bunched muscles of his wide back and shoulders. She didn't want cloth. She wanted taut, velvety skin. This frenzied kissing, the hard caressing, wasn't enough. Her body lolled against his in physical abandon, her skin damp with exertion.

"I want you," he murmured into the hollow of her neck. "So badly I'm mad with it!"

The depth of feeling in his voice was impossible to mistake. She clutched his face between her two hands, trying to force him to confront her. "How can you care about me when you're going after Sonia?"

"What?" He searched her face as though her words had no meaning.

"Experienced women are more your style, aren't they? They know how to play the game."

He stared at her, his mouth set in a contemptuous line. "You've really gone over the edge."

"If I have, you've pushed me."

His eyes actually glittered. "A few kindnesses to Sonia, and you're full of jealousy and malice. Who would have believed it?"

"It's *your* behavior that needs looking into," she cried, enraged.

"Not by *you*." He swung away from her as though he couldn't bear to hear another word.

"Hell, oh, hell!" Rachael muttered beneath her breath. In the end he always made her feel she was to blame. What her father used to call "turning the tables." Curt Carradine had it down to an art.

AN UNEASY PEACE reigned over the house. Sonia abandoned her openly unkind attitude toward Midge, making several attempts to draw her out—an exercise that only succeeded in making Midge more uncomfortable. To divert the younger woman, Rachael suggested they put up the Christmas tree. It was brought down from the attic and assembled in the drawing room, where it towered almost to the high ceiling. The two derived a lot of pleasure from decorating it with the beautiful baubles the family had acquired over many years. Some of the ornaments were quite valuable, and it always seemed that Sonia made a quick foray into the room at the precise moment Midge was endeavoring to fix one in place.

"Why does she do that?" Midge wailed. "I get so nervous!"

That was the whole point, Rachael thought. Finally they were finished, and Scott climbed the high stepladder to place the shimmering white Christmas angel on top.

"Lovely, lovely!" Sonia clapped in genuine delight. "It's marvelous to have you home, Scotty." She glanced smilingly at Rachael. "If you'd like to come with me, I have something to show you."

Wordlessly Sonia led the way through the house to the attic, where she closed the door. It had always seemed to Rachael that the room had a faintly haunted ambience. Although the summer sun burned through the windows, the lighting was strangely dim. As children, she and Scott had terrified themselves coming up here.

Tall pieces of furniture stood, covered in sheets. There were mirrors, camphor chests full of old clothing, a pair of fluted Corinthian columns made of pine, Victorian bric-a-brac, a hundred and one things that had gone out of fashion or the family had forgotten about. There was even the scent of an old perfume trapped in the musty air.

"I swear this place is haunted," Rachael said.

"I have to confess it puts my nerves on edge." Sonia studied her reflection in a long mirror as she passed it. "This is what I'd like you to see."

"What is it?" Rachael inquired with the oddest little shiver.

Sonia glanced back at her with a faint smile. "Can't you guess? Reach in like a good girl. I don't want to get dust all over my clothes." She indicated something stored behind the folded panels of an Oriental screen.

"I hope there aren't any spiders," Rachael murmured, just to lighten the atmosphere.

"It belongs to you, dear, not me, so be brave."

Rachael edged around a three-tiered Victorian whatnot, pressing herself into the narrow space so she could reach behind the screen. Her hand closed over a roll of something. Canvas. She knew before she brought it out what it was. The words died in her throat.

"Go on, open it," Sonia urged. "It's your Christmas present."

"It's my mother's portrait, isn't it?" Rachael stared into Sonia's face. "You denied all knowledge of it."

Sonia lowered her head and nibbled her lip. "Forgive me, my dear. There were reasons. Your father... old memories. I don't expect you to understand. I just hope I've made you happy."

"I'll take it downstairs," Rachael said in a shaky voice. She wanted to open it on her own.

"Do it here. You don't want Midge exclaiming all over it. Here, use the table." Oblivious now of the dust, Sonia impetuously swept a long refectory table clear of assorted silk lamp shades.

Slowly, gently, Rachael began to unroll the canvas as though it was very valuable, which indeed it was to her. She found herself gazing at the portrait of a young woman in a brilliant blue evening gown, seated in one of the Louis Seize armchairs that remained in the drawing room to this day. The yellow brocade upholstery highlighted the rich blue of her dress. Her hands were very pretty. The fourth finger of the left hand was adorned with a wide, lacy wedding band and a magnificent sapphire-and-diamond ring. This was a young woman in the spring of her beauty. Long curling red hair. Blue eyes to match the sapphire. It could have been Rachael's twin, but for a surpassing gentleness about the expression.

"She's beautiful!" Rachael breathed, aware she was trembling. "How is it she's out of the frame?"

"I'm afraid I did that," Sonia offered without further explanation. "Never mind. I'll get it replaced. I'm not proud of a few things I've done in the past, but I wanted to please you this Christmas."

"You have, Sonia," Rachael said, looking wonderingly at the radiant canvas. "This means so much to me. I have so little of my mother."

"Give me the Meissen figurine, too. I'll have it repaired. There's only one thing I ask of you, Rachael. Don't go to Carrara Christmas Day."

Rachael had no intention of going, but still she asked, "Why?"

Sonia smiled rather feebly, took a deep breath and said, "Bizarre as it may seem, we're both in competition for Curt."

"And what makes you think you can get him?" Rachael laid aside the canvas and stared directly at her stepmother.

"My dear, I'm way ahead on...certain points!"

Immediately an old scene crossed Rachael's mind. "You mean you went to his bedroom?"

Sonia gazed at her with a rueful expression. "All's fair in love and war, darling. I *thought* you caught me out."

"I certainly didn't mean to," Rachael said with dignity. "I was going downstairs to get something for my headache."

"Don't look so grief-stricken, Rachael." Sonia's voice held deep kindness. "I'm sorry I have to be the one to shatter your illusions. I know how it feels, believe me. I've told you all along that Curt's attracted to me. You see me as your stepmother, your father's widow. Curt sees me as a desirable woman. It mightn't be love he feels for me, but obviously it's enough. Security for me. Miriwin for him. A marriage of convenience, if you like."

CHRISTMAS MORNING Rachael announced that she couldn't go to Carrara. She wasn't feeling well, she said.

"Maybe it was the champagne last night," Midge said helpfully. "That could be the problem, couldn't it, Scotty?"

"There was nothing wrong with the champagne," Scott maintained, disappointment written all over his face. "It was vintage Bollinger. It's not like you, Rae, to be sick."

"I certainly didn't plan it. You mustn't worry about me, Scotty."

"I was looking forward to a fabulous day."

"And you'll have one," Rachael said. "I have a sick headache and my stomach feels queasy."

"Not everyone is good with midnight suppers," Midge said, clearly speaking from experience. "The chocolate torte was very rich."

Sonia came downstairs to join them. She looked absolutely stunning in a pink silk organza dress Rachael had never seen. "You'll be better off at home, dear," she said warmly. "Take my word for it."

"Sure you're going to be all right?" Scott asked again as he was going down the front steps.

"If I get worse I'll call the Flying Doctor," Rachael answered rather tartly.

"Oh, you and your jokes!" Scott came back to kiss her cheek.

"Besides, I don't want to be around when you and Sonia start selling off our birthright."

Scott colored. "Mum's handling it."

"You're prepared to let her?" And yet there was resignation in Rachael's voice.

Scott looked surprised. "You can trust her when it comes to negotiations. She's a lot tougher than you and me put together. I'll have to go, Rae. Can't keep Mum waiting. She has a pretty short fuse."

In her bedroom Rachael stared up at the portrait of her mother. She had pinned it by the extreme edges to the wall. As soon as the holidays were over, she would take it to Brisbane to have it properly framed. She'd see Matt and Wyn at the same time. She missed them badly, missed their love and support.

Wherever she roamed in the room—to the French doors, the fireplace, the bed—the blue eyes in the portrait followed her, smilingly, lovingly. It was an enormous comfort. That sweet face had a lovely soft witchery. Rachael could readily see that her mother would have been hard to forget. It was obvious now just how bitterly Sonia had resented her. A gentle ghost.

To keep up her morale, Rachael changed into a party dress, one she'd bought at the beach boutique. She brushed out her hair. Secured it in a simple chignon. Applied a little cheering makeup. She had no intention of having a miserable day, she told her reflection fiercely. Now, more than ever, she had to think positive. She would if it killed her. In the end, all she had left was herself. But being alone wasn't so bad. In a sense she always had been. No one should start life without a mother.

Rachael was busy in the kitchen preparing a chicken for roasting when she was startled to hear a chopper whirling over the house. She washed her hands quickly, threw a tea towel over the chicken and rushed out onto the veranda, staring up.

Carrara's bright yellow helicopter was about to land on the home gardens. She was amazed. No one had ever thought of landing right on their front lawn before. She retreated indoors, wondering what to do. Someone had come to check on her. She looked anything but ill. In fact she looked full of an adrenalin-packed energy. She rushed back onto the veranda just as the rotors were slowing to a halt. Another minute and the pilot stepped down onto the grass.

Curt. Who else? He just had to take charge. Rachael felt her chest rise and fall in agitation.

He came up the steps, studying her from head to toe. "Now that's what I'd call a quick recovery," he said cynically. "Midge made me feel I should bring a doctor—only I know you too well."

"I'm sure you don't."

"And you've made the table so nice, too!" He glanced sideways to where Rachael had set things up. A mass of pink and yellow lilies smiled sunnily from a basket. She had tied ribbons to her chair. The tablecloth was of Irish lawn with a deep fringe of lace. China, silverware, wineglass were of classic design. It was Christmas, after all. She deserved some beauty, some pleasure—and she had a lot of trauma to combat.

"You certainly like to do things in style," he said in a sardonic voice.

"This hardly compares with the preparations over at your place."

There was a minute's silence before he spoke again. "Your word obviously doesn't mean anything," he finally said.

"I'm sorry to be constantly disappointing you," she said ironically.

"Don't press too hard," he warned.

"Look, I'm sorry I didn't apologize personally, but I didn't want to disturb you Christmas morning. Now that you're here, would you like a glass of sherry? A piece of fruitcake?"

"You made up the whole thing, didn't you?" he asked.

"About what?" She had to steel herself not to burst into tears, she was hurting that much.

"The headache. The upset stomach. There's not a damned thing wrong with you."

"I made a miraculous recovery after they left."

His golden eyes blazed. "It's important to insult me?"

She held her ground, staring up into his face. "Listen, Curt, at one time I would have been greatly honored to spend the day with you, but things have changed...."

"How, exactly?"

Rachael turned her face away. "I don't want to talk about it."

"It has to be something to do with Sonia."

"You're getting close!" she jeered.

"They're going to approach me about buying the property?"

"You don't *know?*" Her eyes flew to his, scorn in their depths.

"Rachael," he said harshly. "We've had this conversation a dozen times before. I'm sick to death of it. In fact, I'm not sure you're entirely sane on this issue."

"While you're fanatically sane, aren't you? You've got Sonia in love with you, only Sonia isn't as attractive as Miriwin. I'm—"

He seized her suddenly by the shoulders. "You're out of your mind!"

"I *saw* her coming out of your room."

"You really are insane." He sounded disgusted beyond endurance.

"Okay, how do you feel about this—"

"Please, no more!" He released her so abruptly she rocked. "I have absolutely no idea what you're raving about."

"That's what depresses me most!" she cried. "You keep lying and lying. Curt Carradine! Who would have believed it?"

"Rachael, I'm leaving," he stated, turning on his heel. "Have a nice day in the madhouse."

She ran down the steps after him. "The worst thing is you keep making passes at me!"

"Obviously a terrible mistake!" He faced her with clenched teeth.

"Don't you feel any sense of shame?" She threw up her arms, her expression a mixture of pleading and rage.

He shrugged. "No, but then I might be cracking up, too. You have that effect on me. As a matter of fact, I have concerns about the whole family."

"Then keep away from us." She lifted a determined chin. "From *me*, anyway!"

"I would say that's absolutely essential."

She ran after him again. "It's just possible you're driving *me* mad. I can't understand you. I'm nearly—"

He swung back so fast she slammed into him and he held her by the elbows. "Spit it out, Rachael. It's your very last chance."

"You're cracking my bones."

"I'm sorry." He relaxed his grip but didn't let go of her. "Tell me."

"The night before I went into the hospital, remember? I slept until daybreak and woke with a splitting headache. I couldn't find the painkillers, so I decided to go down to the kitchen. Wyn has everything you can think of in her medicine chest—''

"Could we get to the point?"

"I saw Sonia come out of your bedroom and scurry off down the corridor to her room. She was wearing a nightgown and robe."

"That's interesting," he said with extreme sarcasm. "What was *I* wearing? Or didn't you catch a glimpse of me?"

Rachael shook her head. "I didn't see you at all."

"But naturally I was there?"

"It was half-past four in the morning."

"You didn't wonder if perhaps I hadn't gone to bed?"

"I was certain you *had.*"

His remarkable eyes flashed. "And Sonia came looking for me?"

"I don't think it was for a chat."

Once more he threw her off. "That's obscene!" He strode to the helicopter.

"What was I supposed to think?" Rachael stood in the thick grass, almost wailing.

"That I have integrity," he shouted. "That I don't go around seducing the widows of my friends. In their own homes, too!"

Rachael sprang across a garden bed like a gazelle. "You're saying you weren't there?"

He looked at her with magnificent contempt. "I'm not saying anything at all. I'm on my way."

"I was shocked! Can't you understand that?"

He rounded on her, his face filled with outraged dignity. "You seem to suffer from paranoia. You're such a hypocrite, too. Thinking as you do, you must despise me—yet you let me kiss you more than once."

"Do you think I don't feel guilty about that?" Rachael cried. "I used to worship you, Curt."

"I don't need worship, Rachael," he returned cuttingly. "I'll settle for respect."

Rachael turned on her heel and ran back to the house. Later she ate her solitary Christmas dinner without tasting a thing.

CHAPTER EIGHT

THE FAMILY ARRIVED HOME just after dusk.

"We've had a marvelous time!" Midge told Rachael. "The only thing that spoiled it was you weren't there. Carrara is splendid, isn't it? An outback palace. And Curt is such a prince!" She threw herself into an armchair, chattering on happily.

Sonia, on the other hand, had gone straight to her room, rather quiet and white-faced. Now she floated into the library looking frailer than usual, and heavy-eyed.

"Have you been in my room, Rachael?" Her tone suggested she was worried about something.

"I never go into your room, Sonia, unless I'm asked."

Sonia thought about that for a minute. "It's just that something is missing from my dressing table."

"What, Mum?" Scott asked.

Sonia's face betrayed concern and dismay. "My opal-and-diamond dress ring. I wore it the night Curt came to dinner. Remember?"

"You've put it down somewhere, Sonia," Rachael said. "I'll come and help you look if you want." Rachael got to her feet. "Sometimes a thing can be staring you in the face and you can't see it."

"I'm particularly fond of that ring," Sonia said in a distressed voice. "It would be dreadful if I've lost it."

The Munros had not shared a bedroom. They had shared a suite with a connecting sitting room. Alec Munro's bedroom had been decorated in dark masculine tones with a magnificent old rug on the polished floor, comfortable leather armchairs and a collection of architectural prints on the wall; the sumptuous decor of Sonia's ultrafeminine bedroom created an effect of pure glamour. A gilt-framed mirror and console faced the bed. Gilt furniture was everywhere, and the four-poster bed was cocooned in ivory silk draperies. Even the dressing table was dressed in a skirt of white silk, organdy and big, creamy bows. The ring could easily have slipped into the folds. Rachael went straight for it, gently shaking out the silk.

"I've looked there, Rachael," Sonia said a little testily.

"Could it be in your jewel box?"

"Look there if you like. It's on the bed. I truly hate losing things. Especially valuable things...."

"Listen, it's not lost yet," Rachael said. "There's been absolutely no one around."

"Except Midge."

"Let's keep Midge out of it!" Rachael said firmly, letting her gaze run over ropes of pearls, earrings, rings, brooches, enough to encourage any jewel thief to take a trip to the outback. "Gosh, I never knew you had so much. Get it back into the safe. No one but you knows the combination."

"No ring?"

"No opal ring," Rachael said. "When did you last see it?"

Sonia swept her hand through her short blond hair. "It's been on the dressing table, I know. Look, I don't like to say this, Rachael, but Midge seems very... acquisitive. She really embarrassed me the way she gaped and gawked at Carrara. Did she think we lived in mud huts?"

"Not Midge, Sonia," Rachael said very quietly.

"She could have peeked into this room. I wouldn't put it past her. She probably had no intention of doing anything more than that, only she spotted the ring."

"Oh, Sonia, forget it."

"I'm sorry, my dear, I can't. I know all about the haves and the have-nots. Don't forget how Julia Radford had her tennis bracelet stolen by casual help."

"Midge is a guest in this house and absolutely trustworthy."

"How would you know?" Sonia asked in a cynical voice. "She's almost a stranger. You know nothing about her. The fact is, she's dazzled by a display of wealth. Even you can't deny that. I suggest we look through her room."

Rachael actually recoiled. "I can't do that, Sonia."

"I suppose Midge was counting on that. Theft *is* sordid. Do you think I should go downstairs and ask? No, I'd rather check her room. You can come along if you like. It's *my* ring, after all. No skin off your nose if it goes missing."

The door to the yellow guest room stood open. Sonia swept in, followed by the reluctant Rachael who felt obliged, if only for Midge's sake, to be there.

"Untidy creature, isn't she?" Sonia murmured, clicking her tongue in disgust. Midge's untidiness consisted of a forsaken dress draped over a chair and a pair of bedroom slippers sticking out from under the yellow bedspread. "Not the sort of girl you'd want for a daughter-in-law." She made a swift, almost professional search of the Victorian dressing table and drawers. "Nothing here," she said, sounding disappointed.

"Just as I told you. Let's leave. This is a massive invasion of privacy."

"What rot!" Sonia snorted. "This is plain common sense. Check the bathroom. Be quick. Then we can be out of here. I don't want the girl to be guilty, Rachael, jarring though I find her. I don't want to hurt my Scott."

She sounded utterly sincere, so Rachael moved to the vanity. She couldn't bear to touch anything. This was wrong. Midge had left her makeup strewn all over the pink marble counter. The fanatically tidy Sonia would be bound to make a comment. Rachael was just turning away when her eye fell on a speck of darkest blue in a glass bubble that held pastel-colored cotton-wool balls. She slumped against the counter, trying to decide whether she had the right to put her hand in and check. Once focused on the spot she could catch a wink of green. It wasn't a trick of the light. Something was in the glass bubble.

Sonia came to the bathroom door. "What a terrible detective you'd make. Come away, Rachael. I should have spared you this, but I had to tell someone. What on earth are you staring at?"

"The soaps need topping up."

"She probably stole them, too," Sonia said unpleasantly. "What a truly messy girl! You didn't shift anything, did you? I don't want her to find out." She glanced over the counter, preparing to leave when suddenly her hand shot out and closed over the glass bubble bottle. "Thank God my eyes are sharp enough to see what yours can't. There's something in here, Rachael. Unless I'm very much mistaken..." Sonia removed the lid and thrust her small hand into the jar. "What did I tell you? How little we know of people." She slid the opal-and-diamond ring onto her finger.

"Oh, God!" Rachael moaned. "I don't believe anything that's happening around here."

"You're absurdly trusting. On the other hand, I know human nature. One simply can't put temptation in front of penniless young people. In a way, it's my own fault."

"Maybe it's your own doing, as well?" Rachael said, her mind jumping to other conversations with Sonia. "You did say you'd find a way to get rid of her."

"Like this?" Sonia gave a harsh, choking laugh. "Credit me with some decency, Rachael. I'm Scott's mother."

"That's what I mean. If I'm wrong, Sonia, forgive me, but this sort of thing has been done before."

"Most crimes of theft have. All crime, for that matter. Come downstairs with me, Rachael, and we can confront Midge. She'll be given every opportunity to explain herself."

Reluctantly, Rachael trailed after her stepmother. She kept her distance when Sonia confronted Midge about the discovery. Midge went into shock. She sat speechless, staring at Sonia with all the healthy color drained out of her face.

"What the hell are you on about, Mum?" Scott demanded, leaping out of his chair and going to stand behind Midge.

"Darling, this gives me no pleasure," Sonia said sadly. "Your own sister found the ring."

"What?" Scott rounded on Rachael in disgust. "You mean you searched Midge's room as though...as though she were a common thief?"

"Trust you, Sonia, to turn things around," Rachael muttered.

"Don't blame Rachael, Scott," Sonia said. "Midge *is* a common thief. It's not so unusual. Young women shoplift all the time. Especially young women from...deprived backgrounds."

Scott went down on his knees, gazing into Midge's stricken face. "Don't sit there like that, Midge. You didn't touch the ring. Did you?"

"I'm going to be sick," Midge mumbled. "Sick... sick..."

"Not here on the carpet!" Sonia looked down wildly at the Kerman rug.

"Midge, please," Rachael went to take hold of Midge's arm. She helped her rise to her feet, and they rushed to the powder room where Midge was violently ill.

"Aah! Aah!" she moaned, splashing her face, mindlessly, endlessly, water going everywhere, as though she endeavored to wash away the whole terrible incident.

Rachael handed her a fresh towel, her heart torn. "Midge, I'm so sorry."

"Are you?" Midge rasped. She pushed Rachael out of the way and ran from the room.

By the time Rachael arrived in the hallway Midge was flying up the stairs, her long legs racing along the gallery, making for the dubious sanctuary of her room.

Sonia and Scott, hearing the commotion, rushed into the hallway.

"Go up to her, Scotty," Rachael shouted. "You damned near accused her of taking the thing."

"*Who* did?" Scott shouted back, his golden tan faded with shock and dismay. "You, me, Mum? She never once denied that she took it!"

"She's not the first girl to give in to temptation, or the last," Sonia said. "I won't do anything about this, Scotty. Tell Midge I'm happy just to have the ring back."

"This is all too convenient," Rachael said, flushed and feeling guilty. "Give Midge a chance to talk."

"Hell, Rachael, we did give her a chance," Scotty responded, apparently convinced Midge had done it. "I even begged her, but she couldn't get out one word."

"She's in shock. She's a mild-mannered girl—not a trained con woman. I feel very badly about this."

"Don't cast *me* as the villain, dear," Sonia drawled.

"You should have locked the damn thing away, Mum," Scott said with disapproval. "Midge probably had never seen anything so valuable before."

Rachael's blue eyes blazed fire. "Have you got so little trust in her, Scott?"

"You know all about trust, do you?" Scott's face was red with embarrassment. "Why don't you talk to Curt about trust?"

It hit home. "Go to her, Scotty," Rachael told him bleakly. "Things aren't always the way they seem."

Scott raced up the stairs. A few minutes later he put his head over the balustrade. "She won't answer. She's locked herself in her room."

"What an extremely odd girl!" Sonia said complacently.

"Maybe she's fainted?" Scott was completely out of his depth.

"Don't be a fool, darling. She's hiding her head in shame."

"Maybe she's not the only one who should," Rachael said tartly.

BY MORNING Rachael felt compelled to act. She was distressed beyond measure by Midge's racking sobs, which had continued through the night. Midge had great confidence in Curt, and Rachael didn't want to, not after yesterday, but someone had to make a phone call. Only Curt could act as intermediary. Sonia was very much against involving him; hollow-eyed and ashen, she called it madness. Scott, on the verge of collapse, was all for it.

Curt himself answered the phone. He sounded amazed she had the temerity to ring him. Undaunted, Rachael plunged into her request. "I wouldn't ask for me, Curt. It's Midge."

"Surely locking herself in her room is rather childish?" He spoke sardonically, as though it were little more than a storm in a teacup.

"Please, Curt. I can't speak on the phone, but it's serious. I . . . we need you."

A long silence. "Are you sure about that?"

"Absolutely!" Rachael breathed in heartfelt tones.

"I'm coming, then."

When he arrived at the homestead, Sonia appeared at the top of the staircase, one small hand pressed to her heart. "I'm so sorry you have to be involved in this, Curt. It's not my doing. I'm going back to my room. I absolutely cannot take any more shocks."

"So what's the story?" Curt asked as Sonia drifted away. His gaze was shrewd. "Have Midge and Scott had a lovers' tiff? They seemed happy enough yesterday. But you never know with the Munros."

"Not a tiff," Rachael sighed. They began to walk upstairs and she launched into the whole sorry affair.

Scott was sitting dejectedly in the chair outside Midge's room. He jumped up as soon as Rachael and Curt came into sight. "Thanks for coming, Curt," he said earnestly. "We're having no luck at all with Midge. She . . . she told me she hated us."

"I daresay she does," Curt remarked in a dry voice. He tapped on Midge's door, calling out. "Midge, it's Curt. May I come in?"

Midge hurled herself at the door like a hostage on the brink of release. She released the lock and opened the door a few inches. "Thank God you've come!" she cried hoarsely. "I want to get out of here."

Curt was with her about fifteen minutes. When he emerged, brother and sister looked at him anxiously. "Did you learn anything?" Scotty beseeched.

"Yes. She's been pretty badly mangled. Especially by you, Scott. Midge denies she had anything at all to do with the missing ring. I have to say I believe her. She realizes she didn't defend herself as she should have, but she said she was too shocked and wounded. She wasn't prepared for you to doubt her."

"But Curt! There was no one else!" Scott struggled to answer.

"Are you sure about that, Scott?" Curt asked with no expression. "The incident did succeed in breaking you up. Midge wants to come back with me. She's very emotional at the moment. She wants to go home to her parents. No, Scott, don't go in." Curt held out a restraining arm. "She doesn't want to see you for the moment. You won't gain anything, believe me. Maybe in time Midge will see things differently."

"You mean she won't stay?" Scott asked incredulously, brushing his blond hair back with shaky fingers.

Rachael looked at him in astonishment. "Would you, if someone had called you a thief?"

"But I didn't call her a thief!" Scott protested. "All I asked was had she touched the bloody thing."

"She didn't see it that way, Scott," Curt told him in a not unkind voice. "Now, I have guests. I'd like to return to them. Rachael—" his brilliant eyes dropped to Rachael's subdued face "—I suggest you help Midge pack. She won't mind."

Midge was lying on the bed, quiet and composed. "Why did she do it to me, Rae? I didn't think she hated me that much."

Rachael moved to the bed and picked up Midge's hand. "She doesn't hate you, Midge. How could anyone hate you? Sonia is a very possessive woman and she's going through a bad time in her life. She's not going to surrender Scotty to anyone. Not just yet, and maybe not for a long time. You must forgive me my part in it. Believe me, my heart wasn't in it."

Midge turned her head staring solemnly into Rachael's eyes. "She'll hurt you, too, you know."

"No, Midge, that's all over. Don't be too hard on Scotty. Sonia has never been anything but generous and indulgent with him."

"Which is bad news for any girl he gets involved with. As for me? I'll never forgive him."

And Rachael didn't doubt that was exactly what she meant.

When it was time to leave, Scott raced out into the hallway to make an impassioned appeal to Midge to stay. Midge treated him to stony-faced indifference. Sonia had kept well out of the way, preferring the opulent sanctuary of her room. It was Rachael who got behind the wheel of the Jeep to run them down to the airstrip, where Curt would be waiting with one of his small planes.

At the last moment Midge burst into tears. "Why didn't I confront her, Rae? Why the hell didn't I?"

"I can easily turn the Jeep around," Rachael offered, more than willing to. "I wouldn't have let her get away with it."

"For a lady to do such a rotten thing!"

"She might be my stepmother, Midge, but she's no lady. No *real* lady, that is."

"But she's clever. She can twist words. I'd probably come off second-best. Again."

"Don't let it make you bitter, Midge. You're not to blame for anything."

"Except trying to take her son. Boy, I've heard about mothers like that!" Midge bent to kiss Rachael's cheek. "Thank you for the visit. A lot of it I loved. Take care, Rachael. You know now your stepmother can be dangerous. And she's got quite a thing about Curt. Too bad if he cares about you."

"Good luck, Midge."

"You, too." Midge turned and made a dash for the plane.

Curt finished his flight check and came over to Rachael. "Another one of life's lessons."

"If only there was some way I could make it up to her!"

An ironic smile moved his mouth. "I think Midge might settle for a lucky escape. Scott has a lot of growing up to do. As have *you*."

SONIA STAYED in her bedroom until lunchtime, when she emerged in search of a cup of tea. Rachael was waiting for her. "I'd like to talk to you, Sonia, if you don't mind."

"Not about that wretched girl!" Sonia sank into a chair, burying her face in her hands. "I've had just about as much as I can take, Rachael."

"I'm sorry, Sonia, but we must have this out. Midge says she's innocent. I believe her." She paused. "So does Curt."

A thin smile crossed Sonia's face. "C'mon, Rachael. It was too embarrassing for him to say otherwise. I don't think I'll ever forgive you for involving him. This was family business, yet you exposed us all."

"Exposed *you*, don't you mean? It was terribly cruel what you did to Midge. You picked your mark. A more confident girl would have taken you on like you deserve."

Sonia's face reflected her bitter resentment and anger. "How dare you, Rachael?"

"You planted that ring, didn't you? You set up the whole thing. It's an old ploy, but somehow it worked."

There was no guilty reaction from Sonia whatever. She looked across at Rachael with open scorn. "My dear, I asked you before not to make me out the villain. Midge and I worked out the ploy, as you call it, *together*. She had to have some reason to leave the house, and being accused of theft supplied it. In reality I offered her the ring if she'd simply go away. She's obviously never owned anything valuable in her life. The ring is worth many thousands of dollars, as you know. In short, I bought Midge off. Is that so wrong? She was hopeless for Scott."

Rachael stared at her. "How many accounts of this are we going to have?"

"I don't suppose you know Midge has done something like this before?"

Rachael made a sharp dismissive gesture. "Another lie?"

Sonia shrugged. "Ask Scott. He was the one who told me. It seems she has a habit of picking up things. A girlfriend's expensive scarf, a borrowed dress, a handbag, that sort of thing. Things she acquires and never returns. Some people do it with books. Bower birds, I call them."

Rachael shook her head. "Even if it were true, which I doubt, it's not the same as stealing a valuable ring."

"That's *your* opinion, my dear. Stealing is stealing in my book. Believe me, we're well rid of her."

"I *will* ask Scott," Rachael said.

"Do so, by all means. Scott knows his mother doesn't lie. It's my word against a stranger's, Rachael, yet you chose to believe her."

"You told me yourself you wanted to get rid of her."

Sonia nodded wearily. "And I did!"

"So where's the ring?"

"Ask Curt to check her pockets. She's got it, Rachael. I may play hard, but I play fair. I had no idea she was such a consummate actress. Yet remember the day she was playing up to Curt? What a transformation!"

"You ought to start writing novels, Sonia," Rachael said disgustedly. "I'm not swallowing any of this."

"Have it your own way, dear!" Sonia's expression was a mixture of detachment and black humor. "You've got a lot, lot more to learn about life. Midge is probably laughing right now. I was right about that girl all along."

"Why would she want a ring when she could have had Scotty?"

"It wasn't at all certain she was going to get Scott. Why am I wasting my time on this, Rachael?" Sonia cried, her voice rising with frustration. "I can see what you're trying to do. You're trying to discredit me with Curt."

"The hell I am!" Rachael said, thrusting back in her chair. "He wasn't your lover, either!"

"Darling, you'll never know, will you? Incidentally, the sale will go ahead. It was a deal Curt found impossible to refuse. I guess his grandfather will be laughing, wherever he is."

Rachael's blue eyes darkened. "I don't imagine Dad will be doing the same, but in a way it was *his* decision, after all. Dad, despite everything, sold us out."

"You could say that," Sonia agreed. "I think I'll go away in a day or two. The Radfords are pressing me to join them. I'm taking Scotty, too. He's agreeable now that he's not going to New York. No contract will be drawn up until the accountants' report is in, but providing the price is right Curt will buy. I have his assurance. Don't sit there with a long face, Rachael. It gives me indigestion. We can't return to the good old days, dear. Miriwin is lost to you. Maybe it's not such a great loss. Your father led a very hard life. I don't want it for my Scott."

"No, you just want the money. Scott, too. You were never a Munro, were you?"

The look Sonia gave her stepdaughter was pitying. "No, I just happened to be married to your father. Scott isn't a Munro, either. Life isn't going to be a struggle for us, Rachael. Or for you. You're not being turned out into the street. With any luck you should pick up a cool million after we pay off our creditors. More, if Scott goes through with his plan to increase your stake."

"It's the least he can do," Rachael said flatly. "What's more, I'm going to take it. And someday, Sonia, he's going to find out about you."

"What does that mean, exactly?" Sonia's apple-blossom skin flushed.

"That you lie and lie when it suits you. So much is falling into place now. However did you think you could con

Curt Carradine into marrying you? He told me you're the widow of a friend, that's all, and—"

Anger and shock spread across Sonia's face. She slapped her hand down hard on the table, making the cups and saucers jump. "How dare you speak about me? Have you no loyalty?"

"I did, Sonia, for a very long time. You counted on it, but you've finally killed it all. You've been manipulating me from day one. Even if you couldn't land Curt, which you never could, you were going to make darn sure he didn't end up with me."

Sonia burst out laughing. "How's that for wishful thinking, darling! I've known his feelings about you all along. Common old garden-variety lust. I tried to warn you. As it is, you're going to find him very hard to get over."

"What about you?"

"My dear, would I ever confide in you again? No, Rachael, from now on I'm going to play my cards very close to my chest."

Rachael pushed back her chair and got up from the table. "Don't bother. You're the only one who cheats around here."

EVENTS FOLLOWED SWIFTLY after that, as though the incident with Midge provided the catalyst to determine future actions. Both Sonia and Scott insisted that Midge was guilty—of stealing the ring or accepting it as a bribe, Rachael wasn't clear. Both seemed convinced that selling Miriwin to Curt was the best course to follow. That left Rachael the odd one out, but finally she had to accept that she'd been fighting a losing battle. Sonia and Scott united were too powerful for her. Miriwin would pass out of the family forever. Just another grief she had to learn to live with. As for Midge's guilt? She would never believe it. Apart from her instinctive liking and trust for the young woman,

Midge's denial had the unmistakable ring of truth. Sonia's performance, on the other hand, had been just too perfect, almost rehearsed, and the outcome far too convenient. Sonia had always been a conniver. Rachael could bear witness to that. Sonia worked exclusively toward her own ends. That was her nature.

On the morning Sonia and Scott were to leave on the first leg of their trip to Sydney, Scott tried to explain his jumbled feelings to his sister.

"You'll have to forgive me, Rae. I know I told you I was prepared to give things a go, but Mum convinced me my life wasn't here."

Rachael kept her voice deliberately quiet and calm. "One day, Scotty, you might regret it. Have you thought of that? One day when you have children of your own? One of them could very well be a Munro with the land in their blood."

"I suppose." Scott stood on the veranda staring out across the main compound. "Miriwin *was* a future. Of sorts. As for any kids I might have, they'll have to fend for themselves. I don't really know what I want to do. That was a damned fool idea about going to New York, but I'd like to travel. Roam the world. Now I'll have the money to do it in style."

"Then remember what they say. A fool and his money are soon parted. It would be pretty shocking if you ran through it in a few years. It *has* happened."

Scott looked at her and laughed. "Do you think Mum would allow that? She'll have some investment portfolio worked out. Besides, what's hers will be mine. Something to fall back on."

Rachael turned her head abruptly, focusing on a stand of ghost gums. "Maybe it's all been too easy, Scotty. A case of too much too soon."

Scott was quiet for a moment, considering that. "Don't give up on me, Rae. You're the one with the character, but I try. I'm going to even things up, the way I promised."

"Thank you, Scotty. I feel that under the circumstances it's only fair."

Scott nodded. "Mum's against it, but when you think about it, what *Dad* did was pretty shocking. I'll be a lot happier closing the gap somewhat. I only wish you'd come to Sydney with us. Mum says we'll be welcomed with open arms."

"You're a very handsome young man and you'll be rich," Rachael said dryly. "That counts for a lot with Sonia's friends." She rose from her chair and went to where her brother was standing. She placed her hand over his. "Midge didn't do it, Scotty."

A slight edge in Scott's voice betrayed his own doubts. "Don't start that again, Rae. Midge was probably a bit light-fingered. She implied it herself. All I feel for her is compassion."

"So it wasn't love?"

"Rae, I might fall in love a dozen times. Midge was great fun, but as it turned out not ... top drawer. She made no attempt to defend herself. She wouldn't even speak to *me*. I can't forgive her for that. I can just imagine how you'd react if someone accused you of such a thing. You'd go up like a firecracker."

"That's the red hair. But Midge was no match for Sonia."

Scott flushed and looked uncomfortable. "Don't say any more, Rae. I can't and won't believe Mum set her up. That would threaten our whole relationship. I can't have that. I love Mum. She's never begrudged me anything. Not even Midge, though she didn't like her."

"Ah, well, a son does defend his mother," Rachael said. She sighed, closing her eyes. "Who would have thought this time last year what was to happen to us? Dad. Miriwin lost to the Carradines. The family broken up.''

"Hell, Rae, Curt isn't going to ruin the place. He's a brilliant businessman. As for the family? Nothing is going to separate us, Rae. I'll always be your kid brother. You're everything to me.''

Words, Scotty, Rachael thought, but she stood on tiptoe to kiss her brother's cheek.

IN THE NEW YEAR, Wyn and Matt came home, as much to lend Rachael moral support as anything else. A few days later Rachael received her copy of the accountants' report, shaking her head sadly at the accumulation of facts and figures. Sonia wouldn't get her price now. The station was locked in a downward spiral.

Meanwhile, Rachael plowed ahead with her own plans. She would buy a farm, and Wyn and Matt would help her run it. She had been entranced by the beautiful small farms she'd seen on her holiday. Reared to great distances and freedom, she found the city had little appeal for her. The coast was so lush. All manner of rich produce grew in the rich red volcanic soil—pineapples, papaws, bananas, avocados, citrus fruit. One farm she had visited specialized in ginger and walnuts. The flower farms were especially beautiful. She was adventurous enough to try to start up her own business. She would have a lot to learn, but initially she could get in a good capable manager to show her the ropes. She had to take charge of her own destiny; that was going to take a superhuman effort, though.

The curtain had fallen on a whole way of life.

She had neither seen nor heard from Curt. One of the men told her he was thought to be in Melbourne. Scott rang, anxious because they hadn't heard from Curt, either. "You don't think he could possibly have gone off the deal?''

"Anything's possible,'' Rachael had answered wryly.

Intermittent rains continued. Afternoon thunderstorms built up great towering cloud castles in the sky, fantasy shapes that resembled old galleons in full sail. The country had shed its terrible aspect of glaring heat and aridity. Even the stone-strewn gibber plains were ribboned with multicolored wildflowers. A priceless sight.

Rachael had taken to riding out to Monka Gorge, some miles distant from the homestead. The wide sandy bed of only a few short weeks before had given way to a magnificent lake with a roaring splendid waterfall tumbling from the top of the escarpment. It offered the most perfect swimming hole. Silent, except for abundant bird song, secret, unique. In time the water would recede or drain away, according to the rhythm of the seasons, but for now it was paradise with lilies in flower amid the reeds, and wild passion-fruit blossoms climbing out of every crevice in the rocks. How could she bear to leave this flowering wilderness?

Because of the isolation and the heat, Rachael didn't bother with her swimsuit. Neither cattle nor stockmen came here. The men had been told Miriwin was to be sold, and a few had already left. The rest continued in a kind of limbo while their future was being decided. All felt for Rachael and had told her so. The traditions of the bush didn't die easily.

Rachael left her clothes folded neatly on a rock, then she sought the cool greenness of the lake. The water was softer than silk, exquisite on her naked skin. She struck out for the glorious freshness of the waterfall, lingering inside the tumbling silver curtain, diving under the powerful cataract that penetrated to quite a depth.

As her play went on, she became aware someone or something was watching her. She swept back her hair, staring toward the bank with bright, challenging eyes.

"Who's there?"

A grevillea moved, scattering yellow needles. A man's tall lean body came into sight. He was clad in riding gear, but had obviously tethered his horse. *Curt!* Her heart leapt like a fish.

"Good afternoon, Rachael." He held up both hands. "I come in peace."

"Peace or not, you'll have to go back. I'm not wearing a swimsuit."

"That's okay."

Rachael trod water, trying to fight down the all too familiar rush of excitement. "Wyn told you I was here?"

"Wyn has an almost childlike belief in my gentlemanly qualities. Even so, I'm sure she thought you'd be wearing a swimsuit. Are you going to come out, or am I going to go in? I have to say it looks awfully inviting. We have nothing like this on Carrara." He began to unbutton his pale blue bush shirt.

"Hold it. I'm coming out," she called. "I'd really appreciate it if you didn't watch."

"Actually I don't need my blood pressure to rise any more. You're breathtaking, Rachael, as naked as the day you were born." He moved away to sit on a boulder, his back turned toward her.

Rachael swam swiftly to the shore, then, flesh tingling, made a rush for her towel. The sand was very warm beneath her feet. She wrapped the towel around her sarong-fashion, securing it as tightly as she could. Her hair hung in long glistening ropes, but there was nothing she could do about it.

"You can turn around now."

"Terrific!" His golden eyes gleamed. "Even the towel's not too bad. What if I squeeze the water out of your hair?"

"Don't put yourself out."

He laughed. "A pleasure!" He took her long hair in his hands, wringing it like ribbons of silk. Finally he pulled the red bandanna from around his neck and mopped the ends. "Come and sit in the shade."

"I think I should get dressed."

"For sure, but this won't take long." He held out his hand.

"You're an astonishing man! I haven't seen or heard from you for days and days." She found herself being led to the soft grass skirting the gold sand. Melaleucas swayed above them, dappling the area with green and sun-shot yellow. Honey-eaters, lorikeets and parrots fed on the blossoms lending touches of brilliant color. A blue-winged kookaburra ranged over the lake, diving and coming up with a catch in its beak. All was peace and contentment. Except for Rachael's inner trembling.

"I've been in Melbourne. A mixture of business and pleasure. Wyn tells me Sonia and Scott have moved off."

She looked at him in surprise. "I thought you knew."

"I know now. Sonia didn't contact me."

"How very odd. Scotty was under the impression she had. In fact, he rang me, quite anxious because they hadn't heard from you."

"More of Sonia's little games! I expect she's quite embarrassed over the incident with Midge."

Rachael shook her head. "I'm sure it no longer matters to her."

"And Scott believes her version?"

"Scotty knows which side his bread is buttered on. The accountants' report is in."

"I've only glanced through it," Curt said.

Rachael's full mouth curved down ironically. "You mean you got one, too?"

"Next thing you know I'll buy it."

"I know. I know," Rachael said a little fiercely. "Owning Miriwin has been a bit of an obsession with you Carradines."

"Would you rather the Bannermans got it? Or the Faulkners?"

"That's not an easy one, Curt. There was never a running feud with them."

"And you figure you'd like to keep it going?" He lifted the heavy hair from the nape of her neck, emphasizing the beautiful line of her throat.

"I've learned acceptance, Curt."

"It sounds more like it's been forced on you."

"I was pretty angry. Now it's over. Anyway, Scotty is upping my stake to thirty percent."

"The very least he could do."

"Sonia's against it."

"You'll find that Scott will stick to his part of the bargain."

"Bargain?" Rachael turned to stare at him. The handsome, dynamic, experienced face. "You didn't have a hand in it, did you?"

"I might have mentioned it would be a good thing to do."

Rachael tried not to move. Or breathe. "So it was *you!*"

"You do Scott an injustice. It was simply a matter of pointing out a few things. One day next week we'll fly to Sydney and thrash the whole deal out. My solicitors will be present. You'll have to fix it with yours."

"So, the end of an era," Rachael murmured. "We all have to find the strength to accept things we can't change. But I have plans."

"Let's hear them." He turned sideways so he could stare at her. She was sitting with her legs drawn up, one knee bent, her body leaning forward, as graceful as any ornamental statue. Her expression was serious, introspective, yet she presented a picture of erotic sensuality for all the lack of deliberate provocation. The gentle upper swell of her breasts rose above the level of the towel, pale gold like her slender limbs.

"I'm thinking of buying a farm," she said, without looking at him. "I'm not and never will be a city person."

"You don't have to convince me, Rachael." Casually he tucked a pink lily behind her ear.

"There are beautiful farms in the hinterland behind your beach house."

"You don't know anything about farming."

"I can learn!" Her expression fired, became vigorous. "Wyn and Matt will help me. I can get a manager in until we learn the ropes. I rather fancy myself among the orange groves."

"I can imagine you covered in orange blossoms. The towel's slipping, Rachael."

She took a quick look down. "I must get dressed."

"I'd say so. You're much too seductive as you are. No way to talk business."

She swung her head toward him. "What are you getting at?"

"I've come up with an idea, Rachael. If you're agreeable."

Her blue eyes were fixed on him, dark and perplexed. "Wouldn't you have to discuss it with all of us?"

"No. How would you like to go into partnership with me?"

Rachael rubbed the bridge of her nose in agitation. "I'm not sure what you mean."

"It's simple," he said mildly. "I buy out Sonia and Scott. You keep your share. It's possible we can end the old feud with a merger. Miriwin will be run as a Carradine-Munro venture."

For a split second Rachael thought her heart would break. She shot up precipitously, clutching her towel to her. She looked left and right like a small cornered animal looking for a bolt hole.

"Rachael!" Curt exclaimed, in a concerned voice.

"Don't feel sorry for me, Curt Carradine. Don't ever!" Her indignation grew. How could she be expected to cope when she'd been caught defenseless without her clothes? She rushed over the hot sand and the jumble of mossy rocks without stumbling once. She was desperate to reach that neat bundle. A towering storm cloud was already heralding the downpour to come.

"Rachael—" Curt came after her "—what is it now?"

A shudder went through her. She bent and retrieved her clothes, clutching them to her breast. "Since when have you ever considered *me* as a partner?" she asked fiercely.

"I don't know. For years!"

"What?" She could scarcely believe her ears.

"Why act as if I'm insulting you?"

"Because I'm tired of pity!" she cried passionately. "I don't need it and I don't want it. I'm tired of your playing big brother. I'll find a way to live. Don't you worry about me. I'll have money and I'll have Wyn and Matt. Don't be surprised at anything *I* do."

"Your courage is touching, Rachael, but you haven't heard the rest of the deal."

"No, and I don't want to. I've got enough problems as it is. You're just trying to straighten out a mess Dad created. You know it. I know it. The whole outback knows it. No one's going to blame you for taking advantage of the situation."

"Except Rachael Munro, who's never going to let me forget it."

"I won't be around, Curt, to make you feel guilty. I'm going far away to start all over again!"

"No, you're not!"

She tried to duck, but he seized her, enfolding her in his arms. "I'm not arguing with you, Rachael. I'm stating a plain fact. You and I are going to be partners."

Her heart was pounding in her ears. "I need to know a whole lot more about this before I agree to anything!" She smacked her fists down on his locked arms and in doing so lost a grip on her clothes. They fell to the sand—shirt, jeans, pink cotton briefs—while Rachael cursed helplessly.

"Don't get mad at me," Curt said. "*You* dropped them." The laughter in his voice made her struggle all the more.

"Careful, Rachael," he warned.

"Please, Curt. Let me go." Despite herself she was shaking from head to toe.

"Surely." Immediately he released her, exaggerating his movements. "I didn't mean to give you a hard time."

She bent yet again to pick up her clothes. She felt like having a wild weep; instead, she raced for rising ground where myriad small eucalypts displayed their segmented orange-and-yellow blooms. It took her less than a minute to get dressed. The warm breeze had dried her. Her hair was curling madly all around her face. She brought up her hands and tried to smooth it, but as usual it had a life of its own. *Wild hair,* she thought. *Wild, like me.*

Curt was waiting for her at the water's edge, staring out over the hauntingly beautiful bush scene. The brilliantly enameled parrots were shrieking, drunk on nectar. The whole area was flushed with a new light as the storm clouds built up. They spiraled above the gray, weathered escarpment—purple shot with silver, streaks of pink and a livid green, gloriously mushrooming against the still-blazing blue sky.

"Come here," Curt said quietly, half turning and offering her his hand. She went to him as though programmed, caught up in his force field. "This is *our* world," he said. "Our religion. Our land."

"It's going to be hard to leave it. More, it might *kill* me."

He looked down on her head, stroking the brilliant hair. "Wherever you went I'd only come after you."

Licks of flame wrapped around her. "Don't confuse me, Curt."

"Then I'll make it perfectly simple. I want you to marry me, Rachael Munro."

It was as if she were toppling from the highest point of the escarpment. Free-falling. *"Marry?"* Her voice actually wobbled. "There hasn't been a whole lot to indicate that you *love* me!"

"Then you've led a more abandoned life than I thought," he commented dryly. "I'd hardly kiss just anyone the way I've kissed you. No, you're not as sharp as I thought, Rachael. In fact, you must be the last person to know. I've found you irresistible for years now."

"Curt, I have to sit down," she said abruptly before her knees gave out on her.

"We'll sit together." He lowered them to the sand, putting his arms around her and drawing her back against him. "This has to be a first. Someone stole your tongue?"

She stared across at the cascading waterfall. A rainbow half circled the silver curtain of spray. "As a matter of fact, I'm trying to ward off a heart attack. You sound serious!"

"I am!"

"It's just . . . I don't know what to make of it," she cried in a soft, helpless voice.

"You will in about ten minutes. Rachael, my love," he groaned. He caught up her mouth in a series of small biting kisses that made her faint with hunger.

"Curt!" she begged.

His mouth pressed down on hers so deeply she was compelled to turn into his powerful arms.

After that, all conversation stopped.

"So we're going to be partners?" Curt demanded finally. *"Real* partners? Till death do us part?"

"I promise," Rachael returned reverently, emotion throbbing in her voice. "My beloved Curt! Do you forgive me for ever having doubted you?"

"Nope!" He caught her caressing fingers and nipped them gently with his white teeth. "On the odd night, I'm going to make you pay!"

"Oh? How?" She blushed.

"You're going to have to wait until we're married. Two ceremonies, my love. One in Melbourne, the other Carrara. Two receptions. Agreed?"

"Absolutely! What else for a Carradine? I want Matt to give me away." Rachael settled back dreamily in his arms.

Curt nodded. "He'd be top of the list. He's always been there for you. Wyn, too. There's a place for them on Carrara for as long as they like. Wyn can take over from my current housekeeper, if it suits her. Grace is making it clear it's all too much for her. And Matt would make an ideal supervisor. He'll never go back to hard work."

"You've figured it all out?" she gently mocked.

"I'm very grateful to Wyn and Matt for the way they've looked after you. As for *your* family, it's a bit problematic."

"You mean Sonia?" Rachael asked quickly.

"I don't know that I can condone the lies she's told— particularly the lie she told you, that I'd seduced her. Or words to that effect."

"I think you'll find that when the time comes she'll take herself off overseas," Rachael guessed.

"Fine with me."

"I don't even think we'll see her at the settling up."

Curt lifted her hand and kissed it. "So, Rachael Munro, Miriwin will pass to one of our children. Does that suit you?"

Rachael smiled into his golden eyes, her expression as loving and passionate as his. "Above all things, my love," she said joyously. "There couldn't be a better way." On a surge of elation she reached up and pulled his head down to hers, glorying in the love and desire in his golden eyes. "Now kiss me properly," she invited, softly-voiced.

"Properly indeed!" His arms tightened around her, cradling her strongly. "Don't start what you can't finish," he warned.

Their gazes held as he eased her head back, his so intimate and intense she felt the breath catching in her throat.

"I love you," she whispered. "You're my hero. I can't begin to tell you... to thank you...." A rush of emotion brought tears to her eyes.

"Don't, darling, don't cry," he said. There was such tenderness in his voice that sweetness flooded her body. "I'm going to keep you in my arms and my heart through all the days of our lives."

Over the lake, a magnificent Sacred Kingfisher soared on a down wind, the sun glinting off its brilliant azure blue wings. Neither Curt nor Rachael witnessed the stirring spectacle.

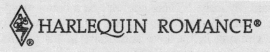

HARLEQUIN ROMANCE®

brings you

Stories that celebrate love, families and children!

Watch for our next Kids & Kisses title in November!

Who's Holding the Baby?
by Day Leclaire
Harlequin Romance #3338

Everybody loves this baby—but who's supposed to be looking after her? A delightful and very funny romance from the author of To Catch a Ghost *and* Once A Cowboy....

Toni's only three months old, and already she needs a scorecard to keep track of the people in her life! She's been temporarily left with her uncle Luc, who's recruited his secretary Grace, who's pretending to be his fiancée, hoping to mollify the police, who've called the child-welfare people, who believe that Grace and Luc are married! And then life starts to get *really* complicated....

Available wherever Harlequin books are sold.